A REGISTRY OF MY PASSAGE
UPON THE EARTH

DANIEL MASON

A REGISTRY OF MY
PASSAGE UPON
THE EARTH

Stories

MANTLE

First published in the USA 2020 by Little, Brown and Company

First published in the UK 2020 by Mantle
an imprint of Pan Macmillan
The Smithson, 6 Briset Street, London EC1M 5NR
Associated companies throughout the world
www.panmacmillan.com

ISBN 978-1-5290-3849-1

1 3 5 7 9 8 6 4 2

A CIP catalogue record for this book is available from the British Library.

Image sources: p. 3, James Gillray, *Mendoza;* pp. 33–37, from Alfred Russel Wallace, *The Malay Archipelago;* p. 57, George Leck, *Group of Boys in Military Costume, Holding Rifles, Flags and a Drum;* p. 79, Ernst Haeckel, *Nudibranchia,* from *Kunstformen der Natur;* p. 99, Édouard Garnier, *Momies de chacal et de chat conservées au British Museum;* p. 117, from Nathaniel Bagshaw Ward, *On the Growth of Plants in Closely Glazed Cases;* p. 147, *Morse's Key,* from Augustin Privat-Deschanel, *Elementary Treatise on Natural Philosophy;* p. 169, John Thomson, *A Comparative View of the Heights of the Principal Mountains and Other Elevations in the World;* p. 201, Arthur Bispo do Rosário, *Large Sailboat,* and p. 227, *Dictionary of Names—Letter A,* photo credit Rodrigo Lopes, Museu Bispo do Rosário Arte Contemporânea.

Acknowledgment is made to the following, in which the stories in this collection first appeared, some differently titled or in slightly different form: *Harper's*: "Death of the Pugilist, Or The Famous Battle of Jacob Burke & Blindman McGraw," "The Ecstasy of Alfred Russel Wallace," "The Miraculous Discovery of Psammetichus I," "The Second Doctor Service," "A Registry of My Passage upon the Earth"; Zoetrope: All-Story: "On Growing Ferns and Other Plants in Glass Cases, in the Midst of the Smoke of London," "The Line Agent Pascal."

Printed and bound by CPI Group (UK) Ltd, Croydon, CR0 4YY

Visit **www.panmacmillan.com** to read more about all our books and to buy them. You will also find features, author interviews and news of any author events, and you can sign up for e-newsletters so that you're always first to hear about our new releases.

For Raphael and Peter

Contents

A REGISTRY OF MY PASSAGE
UPON THE EARTH

DEATH OF THE PUGILIST, OR THE FAMOUS BATTLE OF JACOB BURKE & BLINDMAN MCGRAW

1. Who was Burke? His beginnings.

Born a winter child in the Bristol slums, in the quayside heap known only as "The Rat," Jacob Burke, who would come to battle the great McGraw on that fateful day in 1824, was a son of the stevedore Isaac Burke and the seamstress Anne Murphy. He of Bristol, son of James, son of Tom, son of Zebedee, lifters all. She of Dublin and the cursed Gemini of Poverty and Fertility: Jacob was the twelfth of eighteen children, third of the surviving eight.

It was a common quayside childhood, of odd jobs and shoe shining; of quinsy, croup, and the irresistible temptation of diving from the piers. He grew up quickly. Thick-necked, thick-shouldered, steel-fisted, tight-lipped, heavy-on-the-brow, the boy knew neither a letter nor the taste sweet until his tenth year, when, in the course of a single moon, he learned to sound out the rune on the shingle at Mulloy's Arms and stole an apple from a costermonger on the road to Bath. Two brothers, thinking they were bona fide Dick Turpins, had drifted into a life of brigandage, but by the grace of his mother's daily prayers and father's belt, Jacob turned from the taste of apples and back to the straight and narrow of his bloodline, joining Burke senior on the docks.

And on the docks he remained, lifting barrels of fish and slabs of iron cold from the sea air, until his back broadened and his forearms broke his cuffs.

2. The ascent of Burke, including: the Riots. Also: his early career and its vicissitudes.

At nineteen, Burke became known.

On the quay was a man named Sam Jones, a stevedore too, lifting with Burke from dark hour to dark hour. Sam Jones was an old man of forty when one morning his foot punched a rotted board on the dock and he went down beneath a load of flounder, 150 pounds of fish in an oak-slatted crate that snapped his neck against the railing before he slumped, slipped, limp into the sea.

Sam Jones had a month's wages coming, but the Company

didn't pay his widow, and on the docks, the stevedores sat down and not a boat could move. Then the owners sent out their thugs, who fell on the men with clubs and pokers, and from the melee exploded the Quayside Riots, of fame.

It was a newspaperman from London who first saw Jacob Burke throw a punch. When the riots were over (and Jones's wages still not paid), the newspaperman found him back at the ships, a ninety-pound bag of wheat thrown corpse-like over his shoulder, murmuring a sad low lifter's song as he threaded the sacks and barrels on the pier.

The newspaperman talked a streak. Burke, not accustomed to long converses, let his eyes drift to a seagull hopping on the jetty rail, said *Yes, sir* like he was taught to speak to suits and elders, and occasionally repositioned the weight across his back. At long last the fellow drew out a calling card. *Well? What do you think? Ever fought?* he asked, and Burke asked back: *There's a man's never fought?*

On the card was the name of a warehouse on the harbor, where, over the following week, Jacob Burke sent three men to the floor. They were hard affairs, fighters showing up on the minute as if it were nothing but a shake-bag cockfight. No seconds, no ropes, purse paid out in dirty coins. No Fancy in the crowds, save a smattering of scouts. On the third night came a man Cairn who made an offer.

3. *"Muscular."*

There are nine fights that first year. Hush matches, dueled in warehouses or country inns or levees east of the city. Purses thin, five and ten if lucky. Broughton's rules. Bare knuckles. Twenty-four-foot ring. Round ends when a man goes down. Thirty seconds of rest and the fight doesn't end until a man can't drag himself back to the scratch. No gouging, no biting, no blows below the belt. No faking down to win a rest.

Cairn is his second. Also in his corner, holding his bottle, is an associate of Cairn's, a Yankee who'd once been champion in New Orleans. Yankee must have a Christian name, though he changes the subject when someone asks. He has a crouch, a crablike way of moving, a way of rising to the toes, which Burke thinks are habits of the ring.

They are good to Jacob Burke, these men, treat him like a son. When that winter his father is laid out with cough, they advance him money against his purses. Give him breeches and spiked shoes, read him the fighters' correspondence in the *Weekly Dispatch,* get him victuals when victuals are dear. Buy gifts for his young brothers. Take him to the pushing school, where they tell the girls he will be Champion of England. There, amidst the crepe and taffeta, he is humiliated by the attention, and when they make a show of putting up the socket fee, his face grows hot. Feels like he's back in the ring, half thinks Cairn and Yankee will follow the girl and him, to watch.

Before each fight, Cairn takes him aside and tells him what scum the other is, makes it sound like Burke's some avenging angel, meting out justice to a line of murderers and thieves and virgin defilers. But Burke doesn't really care. He likes the chance to hit and watch his man fall. A ha'penny Bristol rag, with a full page on the fistic, covers his fights, but can't seem to settle on a moniker, calling him the Quayside Brawler, then Stevedore Burke, Bruise Burke, then "Muscular," which Cairn picks up for their promotions. It's elegant, thinks Jacob. He buys a copy of the paper and brings it home, shows his mother which word on the page says "Muscular." He writes it out for her in big letters on a piece of butcher paper, which she folds and tucks into the pocket where she keeps her comb. In celebration, he seizes two of his younger brothers around the waist and lifts them laughing onto his shoulders.

He begins oiling his hair back, which does little for his look except emphasize the weight of his brow. He listens to tales of the professional fighters. He wants to be like Gully so he twists his scarf into a cravat. Purses rise, fifteen and twenty. Buys a stovepipe of the first, and wears it at a rake like Cairn wears his. Like Cairn, who, word comes rumbling, was a walloper, too.

His days of cutting a swell are numbered. In his fourth

fight, his match comes whipping and flapping at him like a fish on the docks. He takes a thumb to the eye and has to spend a week taped up with brown paper and vinegar. Spikes a fever, but Cairn hires a surgeon to bleed him and he's cured.

In his fifth fight, Burke defeats Bristol's Beloved. It wasn't supposed to happen: the fight was an exhibition, a setup conceived to make the champion look good taking down a specimen like Muscular, but Muscular is triumphant.

4. *How Burke came to fight Blindman.*

This is how it came about that Burke fought Blindman:

In Lincolnshire, Broken Head Gall beat the Moor, and in Liverpool, Will Skeggs grassed Tom Johnson, who had no less than the great Peter Crawley in his corner, the butcher's son known in his day as the "Young Rump Steak." But Skeggs wouldn't fight Broken Head, and at Moulsey Hurst, Tim Tate lost to "Le Petit." So Broken fought Petit, but the fight was a cross, the *Weekly Dispatch* breaking the story that both men had met a fortnight before to fix. Then the Fancy went to Ted Shannon the Vainglorious, but Vainglorious knew Blindman and said that if he was going to get killed, he needed a bigger purse for his widow. This left the Fancy still hunting for an adversary, and this left Burke.

The match was scheduled for February, but no one

would post a farthing on Burke. So they called again on Vainglorious but Vainglorious was gone, convicted of thieving and transported. Next, they found a hammer-man in Melchior Brown, from Manchester, who'd been breaking gobs on the tavern circuit under the nickname Sparrow. But Brown went down in just four rounds, and the next pick, Frank Smith the Picturesque, refused to face Blindman's murderous fists. So again they came looking for Burke. They decided Burke's blood would get the Irish out, and Blindman would draw the Scots, and if there was a riot, then all the better. Besides, everyone knew the best fighters wore the Bristol yellow, and by then, Burke had moved out of the warehouse circuit, showing his mettle in a pair of battles at Egan's Abbey.

5. But who is Blindman?

This is Blindman: Methuselah of thirty-five, icon of Scottish pride, hero of boys' magazines, where he was drawn in monstrous proportions, sweeping Lilliputian armies down as if clearing a table for a game of cards. A dexterous hitter of steam-engine power. Won eighteen, lost two. Baptized Benjamin McGraw, he got his nickname in a fight in '14, in the forty-third round, with eyelids so swollen by the punches that he couldn't see. Refused to have them lanced, saying he could beat his boy blind and then leveled him, hard, as soon as they hit the scratch. After the fight, they asked how he'd done it and he answered, *I hit where the breathing was.* He had a patron in the Earl of Balcarres, who was said to slum with him in Glasgow's most notorious. He liked to tell how he'd even been asked to be Yeoman of the Guard, but with all the stories of cursing and rough living and all the girls he'd pollinated, the offer was rescinded. In '16 he'd knocked down the champion Simon Beale in two rounds, and Simon Beale never rose again. In the famous cartoon published in the *Gazette,* McGraw was drawn shaking his fists over a gravestone, on which was written:

HERE IN THE SHADE LIES SIMON BEALE
JAW OF IRON, FISTS OF STEEL
WON TWENTY-FOUR FIGHTS WITH NERVE AND ZEAL
AT TWENTY-FIVE SHOWED HIS ACHILLES' HEEL
TOOK JUST TWO ROUNDS FOR FATE TO SEAL
THAT NO SOUL'S SPARED BY FORTUNE'S WHEEL.

Of course, there wasn't a man among the Fancy who doubted Jacob Burke was going to get lathered. And Burke knew the rumors, but Cairn and Yankee said he stood a chance, that Blindman was growing old, and Burke was improving daily in strength and science.

Truth was, Burke didn't need to be told. And Cairn knew too, for Cairn had been organizing fights for thirteen years, and knew there wasn't anything so proud as a twenty-one-year-old, except maybe a sixteen-year-old, but try to find a neck like Muscular's on a kid. Only problem with Burke, Cairn told him, finger pressed against his pectorals, *Only problem with you* was that Burke was too good and polite and he needed a little more meanness in him. Burke spent a good deal of time wondering about this, about how a hitter could be a good man, and whether he was good only because in the Great Scheme he was on the bottom and he couldn't be anything else, that if conditions were different, he wouldn't be so. Once in a pub he'd heard, *There's no such thing as a sin man, only a sin world,* which he was told meant that the Devil was in everyone and it was a rare fellow who could keep him down. Then, later, he started thinking that maybe he'd heard it wrong, and it should have been, *There's no such thing as a good man, only a good world,* and he started repeating it enough that he couldn't remember if the basic situation was sin or good. Cairn said he was *too good,* but he knew inside that he hit because he liked the feeling of hitting the other fellow, which seemed at first like sin, but then he started thinking that if the other fellow was just like him, then the other fellow liked hitting too, and that meant he, Burke, was pounding a sinner, and so he, Burke, was good, except when he looked at it another way, then the other fellow was also clobbering a fellow who liked hitting (him, Burke), which meant the other fellow was good, and Burke was a sinner for milling an upright man.

The reasoning went round and round like one of those

impossible songs that never stopped, until Muscular decided that what he liked about the fight was that he didn't have to wonder about such questions, only hit, because if you didn't hit, you got hit. That was the answer!

6. *The day approaches.*

So Burke takes to training, docks in the day, dumbbells at dusk. Cairn has him running his dogs in the hills. Hits the bags of sand. Bans drink and the amorous.

The word spreads fast around Bristol, and hush soon follows where Muscular walks. In the streets, he's besieged by shoeshine boys, who beg to see standing flips and then let loose on each other with fists swinging. And the girls... Oh, how they lower their bonnets and lift their eyes when he rooster-swaggers past!

The posters go up, with sketches of the two men facing off as if they had posed together, shirtless, in ankle boots and breeches, tied close with sashes. They say the fight will be held at Moulsey Hurst, southwest of London, but all know this is a sham to throw off the magistrates. The papers take to calling the fight Blindman's Brag, as if it were not a fight, but a showcase for McGraw. As if Burke weren't even fighting.

One night, his mother is waiting for him when he comes home. *They say you're going to get killed,* she says. *Who says that?* asks Jacob. *They all say that,* she says. *I've been to the market. They say: Make sure they promise you the purse, Annie, 'cause your boy isn't coming home.*

Unspoken, but hidden in her words, is his father, who is coughing himself to bones, and hasn't been down to the docks in months. But she doesn't say Jacob should walk away. Had she, then he would have squared his jaw and proclaimed that he had his honor to protect. It is because she says nothing more that the doubts begin to eel their way in.

Except he knows he can't get out even if he wants to. He owes Cairn, for the scarf, for the stovepipe, the food. Cairn says that with the purse from the fight with McGraw, he'll be paid off and then some. Jacob decides *then some* means even more if he wagers on himself. Then he'll stop.

7. *They find a patron.*

Two weeks before the fight, Cairn quarries a patron in a Corinthian named Cavendish; the rest of the fee is put up by the Pugilistic Club.

Cavendish meets Burke and Cairn at Ned Landon's public house. He's a dandy—curls, perfume, and cant jargonic. Wants to be called Cav, but Burke calls him Mister Cavendish, and he smiles. He made his blunt during the Regency, and flaunts it, burns a bill before their eyes. Recites a fight poem which he had published in *Bell's Life,* full of lettery words Burke has trouble getting his ears around. Tells a story about a fighter, laughing, says, *Poor Tom had his eyes knocked from his head. Just like that. Plop. Plop. Couldn't find work and suicided. Drank prussic. Plop.* Burke hates him immediately, feels his whole body tense up when he hears him jaw. He knows Cavendish is trying to look big by making him look small, but he can't think of fast words to answer. Any other man, and he would hit him so hard he'd lose more than his eyes. He looks to his trainer, and Cairn tilts his head, just a little, as if to say, *Easy, son. Swallow the toad. For fame, some things must be endured.*

Ripe, Cavendish begins to slur. Calls a wagtail over and throws an arm around her waist. Tells Burke to remove his shirt. Says, *Look at the symmetry, look at the strength.* Says, *Your mum's Irish?* Calls him *My little boy.* Touches his arms and says, *My, this is pretty.* Drinks his blue ruin until it runs down his chin. Says he was a boxer, but holds his fists with his thumbs inside.

8. They travel to the scene of the fight, spending the night in a coaching inn, where Burke meets a man who imparts his Philosophy.

The fight is set in Hertfordshire, in a field south of Saint Albans called Dead Rabbit Heath. In Saint Albans, they spend the night at a coaching inn. Cairn and Yankee drink until they're reeling, but Muscular is too nervous to keep anything down. The publican is an aficionado of the fistic, and his walls are decorated with sketches and mezzotints of the great fighters, and Burke recognizes Broughton and Painter and the Jews Mendoza and Dutch Sam, and Gasman and Game Chicken. He wants to be like the portraits, still and quiet and distant on a watercolor patch all alone and glorious. But among the rabble that's crowding the tavern, Muscular is cornered by a farrier, a fat, spectacled man who seems to have some reading behind him. Says he was a priest once, which explains his fine diction, though he won't say why they stripped his cassock. *You'll be one of the greats,* he tells Burke, finger to the sky like he's back preaching on his hum-box. *Just look at you. Maybe you'll lose tomorrow but it doesn't matter. Just hold your own, and soon you'll be Champion.* He asks if he knows of the battle between Achilles and Hector, but Burke has never heard of these two fighters. The farrier shrugs. *You ever seen McGraw?* he asks. Burke hasn't, sketches only. *Goliath,* lisps the farrier. *Like someone pressed two men into one. Misshapen like that too. You'll see. Cauliflower ears. Ears? No! Cauliflower face.*

He presses on. *You want to hear my Philosophy? How are you going to win? Think, my boy. You want to win or you want to hurt him? Those are different things. Pastor Browne's theory of the fight is that anger only takes a man so far. That's what all you poor boys start with: anger, needing it like a horse needs a rider. But soon that gets in the way. You boys go out and think you are fighting a boxer but really you're fighting the world. But a good fighter, you see, like Blindman, he knows that the man he's fighting is fighting first to hurt and next to win. And he'll use it. Use your hating to get you. That's the difference. Men who fight to hurt will get it in their time.* Gladiator in arena consilium capit. *He'll finish you. Mill you to a jelly. Get your head in chancery, and then where will you find yourself?*

Burke doesn't have an answer. He stares at the man, who's got whiskers thick as string. The man's going on about anger, and Burke is tempted to say, *There's no such thing as a sin man, only a sin world. I'm just hitting.* He doesn't want to talk anymore. But he won't leave, won't go to sleep either. A tavern chant swells. *Then let us be merry / while drinking our sherry . . .*

He has a sick feeling and thinks that maybe he is scared.

9. They gather at Dead Rabbit Heath.

The fight is to take place another two leagues from the inn, on a field not far from the highway, in a soft depression between the hills.

Soon after sunrise, they take a coach. They pass crowds heading down the road, on foot and horseback. A balloon rises in the distance. There are tents set up for peck and booze. The traffic is slow, thick with carriages. It takes Burke a long time to realize that the crowd is there, in part, for him. They stop at a small clearing halfway up the hill. Burke gets out, followed by Cairn and Yankee. Almost immediately he is set upon by the tag-rag, who jostle to get close. They sing, *Gotta get the Blindman, or the Blindman gets you.* Burke wears his stovepipe low over his eyes, his seconds flank him, leading him up a long path through the wet grass, over a rise and then down toward the ring. Both men hold him by his elbow. He wonders if it's supposed to comfort him. He thinks, Where do they flank men like this? and the answer is the gallows.

As they approach, there's a massive crowd already gathered at the ropes, and he can sense a hushing in the near. They've got two stands set up by the ring for the paying, but the crowds flow up the hills. Now desperate for reassurance, he looks for Blindman, as if the other fighter were the only one who could know what's going on inside his mind. But Blindman is nowhere to be seen.

The ground is turned up like a pack of pigs came rooting through, but the ring is clean, neat, covered with sand, like nothing he's ever fought in. They've strung two lines of painted rope, the scratch is already chalked. He keeps his greatcoat on as Cairn goes and speaks to the judge. He feels the eyes of the crowd on him, tries to ignore them, looks down and keeps clenching his hands. Finally, he lifts his face and looks out. The hill is all men, far as the eye can see. There's a pair of swells near him, silk ties blooming, suits of bombazine, capes, pearl buttons. *Hey, Muscle,* one says and laughs. *I've got money on you, Muscle,* says the other. They're talking funny, and then he realizes they're mocking a brogue.

Cairn comes back. *This's big, boy,* he says. *Ten thousand men, and not a stable free for a sleepy nag. Half the country wants to see our boy fell the champ.*

10. *Cheers and jeers as his opponent approaches.*

Late in the morning, McGraw arrives. Burke hears the murmurs thrumming through the crowd, then shouts going up, the hillside parting for a dark figure surrounded by an entourage. They are far off, descending the opposite slope. For an instant it is as if Burke is watching a shadow at sundown, the dark hulk lumbering over his seconds. A fight song materializes out of the noise, but he can't hear the words. Then suddenly, with McGraw halfway to the ring, something ugly must have been said, for Goliath lunges into the crowd. Then tumult, the black suits turning over as if they were dominoes. Burke can't tell if McGraw is swinging—it's all men coming up and falling back and shouting and flailing like a giant seal thrashing in the surf. Then his seconds must have gotten hold of him, for he's pulled back, and the crowd ripples and is still. Murmurs now: *A beast, they shouldn't let him fight,* but Burke knows he did it for show, though he doesn't know if the show is for him or for the crowd that's come.

There are no more incidents. As McGraw gets closer, a quiet descends. At the edge of the ring, McGraw hands his greatcoat and hat to his second and steps inside. From his corner, Burke watches Blindman strip.

Jacob Burke has prepared himself for a giant, but he doesn't think he has ever seen such a human as this. McGraw must be twenty stone. Six foot six at least, but the illusion of height is increased by the size of his chest and belly, which set his head back like some faraway peak. Arms as thick as Muscular's hams. Fists slung low. Skin pale, blotched red. To call his ears *cauliflower* would be a compliment. *Tuber* is more like it, thinks Burke. Raw tuber that could break a knuckle. Nose the grey-yellow color of a dead man's. There is so much of him that it is difficult for Burke to see what's meat, what's fat: it looks as if someone has taken a massive sculpture of a strongman and kept throwing lumps of clay on it, until the clay ran out. Burke doesn't even know where he will land his fists. It seems like certain rules, like rules against grabbing the throat, don't matter when it comes to Blindman, for Burke is uncertain where the neck ends and the head begins. It is as though he had been told to lift an awkward stone without a place to set his hands.

He knows that he has been seduced by the promotion

posters that show them facing off, as if they were two men fighting. This isn't two men fighting. This is one of the games of gladiatorial speculation he once played as a child: *If a lion fought a bear, if a turtle fought a buck, if a shark fought a giant fox. If an eagle fought a man of fire. Who would win? Who would kill who?*

If Muscular Burke fought the monster McGraw.

It is then that Burke realizes he has been set up to lose, that Cairn and Yankee could never have expected him to stand a chance against Blindman. His pulse skitters, frantic as a droplet in a hot pan. He looks back out at the crowd. Now it stretches all the way to the crest of the hillside. The sound of its chanting is deafening. But he hears only *Blindman,* for they are there to watch Blindman win or Blindman lose. Curse and praise, but only Blindman. The crowd doesn't even seem to see Burke. Thinks Burke: Who cheers the fox, when you've come to watch the hound?

11. *The fight begins.*

The Padders are at the ropes. There are six of them, a quintet of London coal men and an ostler who is retired from the fistic. Their jackets are off, their cuffs rolled, fighting to keep the crowds back. Burke realizes that while he has been lost in thought, his arms loose at his sides, his seconds have stripped him to his breeches.

He stands in a daze. He realizes he's staring into the crowd, looking for someone he knows, another lifter from the docks or—desperate now—a brother, or even his mother, when Cairn whispers something in his ear. He has almost forgotten his second, but now Cairn is behind him, his hands on Burke's shoulders, massaging the massive deltoids of which he is so proud. Burke shivers him off. Is he in on this? he wonders. How much is he being paid to have me get killed? He shakes his head as if there's poison in his ear.

Behind him, he hears Cairn's voice. *Show 'em, Muscular.* He coaxes his arms into the air, and Burke flexes. *That's right, Muscular,* says Cairn. *Show the old man.*

What are the odds? Burke whispers.

Cairn rubs his shoulders. *Don't worry, boy. You do the milling and I'll do the betting and we'll both go home rich men.* He laughs, but Burke doesn't join. No matter how hard he tries to throw his anger back toward the giant in the ring, he feels only fury at his handlers for what's about to happen. The thought that Cairn and Yankee want him to lose vanishes, but what remains is somehow worse, that he is inconsequential. The idea that they could have cared for him any more than a trainer cares for a dancing bear now seems a fantasy he was a fool to have believed. He should sit, lay it down, get back to "The Rat," the quayside, home.

They are called to the scratch. The judge joins the Padders in the outer ring. Burke sees Cavendish in the front row, toppered in a white stovepipe that is immaculately, impossibly clean. Beside him: the jostling bettors, the flit-fluttering fingers of a tic-tac man.

The two fighters shake. McGraw's paws are like the rest of him, geologic, and while Burke has a grip that can shatter a bottle, he cannot even get a purchase on the Scotsman's hand.

Time is kept by a Lord from Essex. The judge launches his cant, promising strength and speed and stamina: *A battle of brawn, a beautiful combat, a most severe contest for the benefit of Honorary Gentlemen.* The crowd erupts.

May the best man win, says the judge.

12. Fists up.

Fists up and in the crouch, Burke can't hear the bell for all the shouting. Before him, McGraw holds his pose, shoulders squared, his face a mask, waiting for the boy to come. Burke wants to strike, but he can't move, can't see a line through the giant's arms. Blindman puckers his lips and kisses the air. The crowd roars. *Muscle, muscle,* comes a taunt, and out of the corner of his eye, Burke sees the two swells laughing, while beside them, Cavendish does nothing to fight off a smile. Off the scratch, and Burke strikes Blindman's jaw. But: nothing. Again he strikes and Blindman stops it with his left. His forearm barely gives. Blindman makes a face of mock surprise, brushes his arm as if flicking off a fly. Flourishes his fists. It's a show for the crowd, and they reward it with thunder. Burke rushes again. Left to Blindman's jaw, but then a brick comes hard against his head.

Muscular down.

Cairn takes him back in the corner, sits him, whispers, *Tire him, Muscular. Feet, Muscular. Quick on the pins. Dance like Mendoza,* but Burke pushes him away, is back to the scratch before the Lord says thirty. Throws a punch the instant Blindman gets up from his corner. *Foul!* he hears, but before they can pull him back, he's down again, unaware of what happened. He tastes dirt this time, hears the judge call *First blood,* and feels his cheek is wet. Hears numbers. Can't distinguish the crowd's shouting from the roaring in his ear.

Back to the scratch and Muscular down.

Back to the scratch. Blindman charges. Muscular swings, strikes to the neck and the giant is down. The hillside roars like artillery fire. Then McGraw is up, his flesh shifting and shimmering. Burke advances. He can't think now. Can only move.

13. The fight continues.

The rounds roll through him. Hook to Blindman's ear. Burke in the mouth. One-two. One-two. Blood, tooth, and Muscular down. Jab to nose and Blindman down. Back to the scratch and Muscular pounds the pudding bag, the ear, the ear, and the ear seems to crumple, break like a potato beneath a heel. Blindman down. Back to the scratch and Blindman rushes. Breadbasket, breadbasket, Muscular down. Topper to the ear and Muscular down. Pirouette, turn, and Blindman rushes. Muscular back, clips a heel, down. Back to the scratch. Fast to the eye, Muscular down. Again to the peeper, Muscular down. Blindman muzzled and Muscular down. Blindman coughs, spits out a grinder. Chop and chop and Muscular down. Back to the scratch and Muscular down. Blindman, Blindman, Muscular down.

Eyelid swollen, tasting blood on his tongue, his knuckles wet with gore, Burke sits in the corner, letting Cairn's hands caress his chest, Yankee sponge his face. He feels as if his men aren't there. He's being touched by bird wings. He wants at McGraw, needs to hit. It hurts to breathe, he doesn't know how much lung he's got left, but something in him says that he's taken the worst. That Blindman's not going to hit any harder than he's hit but that Muscular's still got it, still could heave a load. He murmurs a stevedore's song: *And lift the barrel lift the barrel lift the barrel, hey! / Twelve kittens in the kitchen and another on the way.* His lips, swollen, blubber. He rinses his mouth with Old Tom, rises before the thirty. Is at the scratch before Blindman stands.

By now the crowd is pressing up against the rope, throwing punches at the Padders, curses flying. Again Burke rushes. McGraw catches his wrist this time, turns with the force and throws him, lands with his knee in Muscular's gut. Burke's mouth fills with bile, his pants go wet. He hears hissing and a cry of *Foul,* but McGraw, snorthling through his broken nose, doesn't care, he cradles Burke's head, whispers something rasped into his ear, kicks Muscular in the flanks as he tries to stand. Again, *Foul!* But this is coming from the crowds, closer, and Burke sees a man breach the outer ring, hurling ugly curses at the Scot, followed by another and another, and Burke, up on his knees, thinks, Here we go, and he isn't even standing when the punches start flying.

14. Pandemonium in the ring, at times the two fighters join forces to restore order.

A gasman hits a liveryman hits a brewer hits a baker. Two swells pound the other as if to send him to his maker. An ostler lands a muzzler while his best man lands a quaker.

The Padders overwhelmed, the ropes broken, the crowd implodes. They don't seem to be after the pugilists but one another, though Muscular, spinning, can't seem to make heads or tails of what's happening. There's a mob come down cursing the Scot. There are canes swinging, and stones thrown and someone heaving a rope, and the air is filled with curses, all kinds of animal and things that are going to be done and a liberal use of the Monosyllable.

Then Muscular and Blindman have joined the Padders, pounding to clear the ring, because both are hungry for the fight. Blindman is red-faced and breathing heavy. Rested, Muscular feels the strength in him returning.

By the time the riot is cleared, a dozen men have been carried off. Then the ropes are restaked, the colors returned. A quiet settles, but the judges are still shouting, threatening to end the fight unless order is restored.

15. But what has become of Muscular's eyes?

Time has played Blindman's ally: by now, Muscular can barely see, both of his eyes are swollen shut. With the stage reclaimed and the Padders back at the ropes, the boxers repair to their seconds. In his corner, Cairn runs his thumbs over Muscular's lids. *You're out,* he says. *You're out or I cut them,* and Burke nods. Cairn pushes his head back, grabs the blade, and the relief is immediate. His face streams with the claret, his cheeks feel as if he were crying.

Back to the scratch, and McGraw still fighting dirty,

but the judge lets it fly. The judge is angry, thinks Burke, likely has his own money in this, knows this shouldn't have gone on this long, was supposed to be easy, done. Face contorted, McGraw rushes, gets a hand on Burke's neck, and drives him into the rope. Muscular down. Cairn calls *Foul!* but he's back to the scratch.

Now it's Burke who leads. Forward now, and Blindman back. Fists up and McGraw circles, spits, coughs, scratches the ground. To, fro, Burke forward. Watching watching, and he sees it, sees his gleaming channel in. Not now, but two moves from now, just like a game of draughts. Feels the warmth in his arms, thinks, This is glorious. Feigns high and McGraw goes high and then Jacob Burke is inside. Left to the jaw, left, and Blindman ducks. Straight into Burke's right and rising.

Jacob Burke knows then that the fight is over. Hears it. Something slackening. Something soft, something broken in the jaw or in the cheek, something creaking in the temple. He's worked shipbreaking at times, and there's a feeling when a sledgehammer comes against a beam and nothing breaks, but you know the next time you swing it's going to give. Blindman is standing, but Burke has only to wait and Blindman will fall. An expression comes over Blindman's face, a puzzled expression, like he's hearing a song he's never heard before.

At which point Jacob Burke has a very complicated thought.

16. *Jacob Burke's thought takes the form of a memory.*

In his childhood on the docks, Jacob Burke and his friends spent hours in games of earnest battle, clashing sticks and throwing stones long into the dark, chasing and fighting and raising hell. They played by the universal rules of cruelty and chivalry and thrill, thrill to strike and throw and be thrown at, and throwing and chasing one day, Jacob and three friends had cornered an enemy knight and were taunting him before delivering the coup de grâce, which in such a situation, with such easy prey, typically consisted of tagging him with the stone or tossing it lightly, as the boy was trapped against a wall and had no way to escape. But that afternoon, the boy, who was younger than the rest, went scared on them and started to cry, and, surrounding him, the others began to laugh and throw and then the boy was crying louder, which only made the others laugh louder and throw harder and then the boy was slobbering for his ma, and they all went grabbing more stones and throwing and Burke reached down and felt his fist close around a stone which he knew was too big for that game but the crying had removed from him any restraint, and, laughing, he took hard aim at the boy and threw.

17. The end.

Watching from the crowds, amidst the cheers and curses, there's not a soul that day at Dead Rabbit Heath who knows what Jacob Burke knows: that the fight is already over. For Blindman is standing and Blindman's fists are still up, and if he's slack in the lip no one can see from what Muscular Jacob Burke has done to his face. They'll know, in breaths they'll know, and for years they'll talk about it, but in this half second between Muscular's knowing and the crowd's knowing, it's as if Muscular has been left alone with an awareness and an omnipotence that only God should have.

There is a moment, as a lifter takes a load and heaves it onto his shoulder, when the massive weight, the sack or the crate or the barrel at the top of its heave, becomes briefly weightless, and the lifter, no matter how tired he may be, poised between his action and the consequences of his action, feels both an incredible lightness and the power of the weight at the same time. It is as if he is master of the weight, not struggling below it, and Jacob Burke has learned over the years to seek this joy, cling to this joy, knows secretly that in the misery of everything else, there is one moment when he is king.

Maybe he thinks this or maybe he feels it in the movement of his arms, for now there is no difference between thinking and feeling and hitting.

Blindman's fists are down and Muscular comes in on his man. He is feeling for the break, the hole, the soft, searching again for that seam, hitting, hitting, that half second gone, and now there's no turning back, hitting, knowing that when he'd told himself he hit so he wouldn't be hit, he was lying, because beneath it, the reason he hit is that there was joy in hitting, real joy in the simplicity and the freedom and the astounding number of answers in a single movement of his arms. Later he'll have pity but not now, now there is no pity, not because he is cruel but because there is no more Ben McGraw. For Muscular is alone, mind clear of all but such joy as he moves in, striking his man, searching, knowing there is only one way that he wants this to end, only one ecstatic way for it to end, only one, and hitting he thinks *Blindman I'm hitting Blindman I'm hitting Cairn I'm hitting Cairn I'm hitting Cav I'm killing Cairn I'm hitting Cav I'm hitting Blindman I'm hitting Cav* and then feeling the soft thinks *I'm in the break* thinks *in the crown* thinks *in the line* thinks *into McGraw* thinks *there is a line into McGraw into the soft into McGraw into the crown of Ben McGraw into the temple of McGraw the broken temple of McGraw . . .*

The broken temple of McGraw.

thinks *there is no such thing as a fast man only a slow world*

thinks *break   break*

Blindman down.

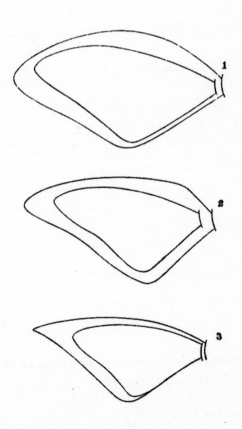

THE ECSTASY OF ALFRED
RUSSEL WALLACE

I wrote a letter to [Darwin] in which I
said that I hoped the idea would be as
new to him as it was to me, and that it
would supply the missing factor to explain
the origin of species. I asked him if he
thought it sufficiently important to show
it to Sir Charles Lyell, who had thought
so highly of my former paper.

A.R.W., *My Life*

He was a man entranced by life's variety. As a child, he
had collected—fossil, flower, beetle, stone—and it was as
a collector that he would come to understand his purpose.
Forced by his father's debts to abandon school in his
thirteenth year, he learned from what he could gather:

broadsheets and belemnites, discarded primers, Milton and *Crusoe*. Let the great men of Oxford and Cambridge proceed with their philosophies. No: the machinations of a Creator with the whimsy to make birds-of-paradise, place hearts on the left, and twist seashells to the right—this was beyond his ken. But the search! The search was his calling. Hadn't a phrenologist told him he would always be seeking? Of the twenty-seven brain organs of Gall, he had large protuberances in *Ideality* and *Wonder*. When he contemplated nature and all her permutations, it filled him with an ecstasy that at times felt like lust.

To Samuel Stevens, his agent in London, he sent his collections, destined for cabinets of curiosities and municipal museums, and from Stevens came the means to finance his expeditions. From Wales, he left for the River Amazon, where bees entangled themselves in his beard and his legs erupted with the bites of the *pium*. In Barra, he hypnotized street urchins. In the slack-water lagoons at São Gabriel, pink dolphins circled his boat. Ants attacked his bird skins, with preference for the eyes. Those specimens he wished to keep whole he bottled in cane liquor, and well into his old age, when he thought of life and its vast diversity arrayed, it smelled to him of spirits. By the time he returned to England at the age of twenty-nine, he had endured the loss of his brother to yellow fever, eight bouts of malaria, the destruction of his collections in a fire on the Sargasso Sea. To such misfortunes, he would add the general indifference of his homeland to his discoveries, his dismissal as a *bug collector* and a *species man*. He swore he would never travel again. In March of 1854, he left once more, for the Malay Archipelago, on a steamer of the P&O Line.

If, in his letters to his mother, he wrote joyfully of where he went, his physical travels were but a faint trail through the vastness of his wonder. Whether he expected great revelations from his early collections, he didn't know; the collections were an end in themselves, the consequences of which he did not consider until the consequences seized him. When he turned, at last, to theory, one thing was clear: he did not intend to destroy faith; he intended to explain the shaping of a beetle's horns. Should faith fall in the process, he thought (and then thought about it no more), it was a matter for theologians to resolve.

And so he was unprepared for the magnitude of the epiphany, when it came, on that spectacularly warm, tropical spring morning in 1858. Indeed, they said he had the naïveté of a child: too trusting, too awed by others' greatness to know that he deserved greatness himself. There were hours when he thought: I know nothing. And there were other hours, chiefly at night, waking from dreams he didn't remember, when a different thought came: that idea, that beautiful burning idea, that recasting and refiguring and resculpting of the world, that idea burst forth from me, and me alone.

★   ★   ★

Later, back among Englishmen, he would say it came to him in a fit of fever. For months he had been traveling, like a nomad, through the shattered volcanoes of the Archipelago: Celebes, Sarawak, Kalimantan. Monsoons greeted his arrivals. In Singapore, he peered into the great cauldrons of American whalers. On Borneo, he shot orangs. His boat needed only to touch shore and he would vanish into the jungles with his net in hand.

He traveled, as he always did, without rest, driven by the constant fear that there were species he would miss, forms and colors he would never know. Racked by chills, thin, exhausted, he could scarcely remain upright for the entirety of his meals, and yet in the field, he moved with the same alacrity as he did during his childhood days gathering windfall from his neighbors' apple trees, powered not by physical strength but by a momentum of mind, movement driven by movement itself, by the sun and heat and cold on his neck, by his astonishment at the natural world unfolding. From life at sea, he had acquired the habit of rising early, from the rivers and countless portages the conviction that one does not own what one can't carry. In moments of reverie, he imagined his body light of all but the clothes on his back and the exquisite catalogue of his mind. He was thirty-four. To his mother he wrote, *I am running out of time.*

Bug collector, species man. It was fitting perhaps that the first fateful communication from Darwin came as a simple request for specimens of Malay domestic fowl. When that letter arrived, addressed from Down House, he couldn't believe that it was real. Surely, he thought, it must be a prank, played on him by a friend! It was only two years before the day that would forever link his name to Darwin's, and yet it was beyond his wildest fancies to think of him as a correspondent. He wasn't twenty when he first read *The Voyage of the Beagle,* and for his entire life, when he thought of its author, he found himself a gangly, bare-chinned boy again. He had read all the great man's works on barnacles.

He sent both a domesticated duck and a wild type from which the domesticated breed derived. And in a fit of boldness, he included musings on a question that had begun to occupy him, namely the appearance of variations among species, about which he had written a single essay, penned on Sarawak, published in the *Annals,* and generally ignored. When at last, in Macassar, after months in the jungle, he received Darwin's reply, he opened it on the docks.

His hand trembled as he read, over and over again:

I can plainly see that we have thought much alike & to a certain extent have come to similar conclusions.

Tears sprung to his eyes. Again he read it, then folded it away and began to walk back to the shore, stopping ten yards later to check his pocket and assure himself that it was there.

I can plainly see that we have thought much alike & to a certain extent have come to similar conclusions. Did he recognize that the letter contained not only praise but a veiled intimidation? *This summer will make the 20th year since I opened my first-note-book, on the question how & in what way do species & varieties differ from each other,* Darwin had written. *I am now preparing my work for publication.* But if there was a warning in these words, it was one he didn't notice. It was impossible that someone so great could see a bare-chinned boy as threatening. Or perhaps, forever a traveler in another's country, he had known too much kindness from the strangers in his life.

And so, in Macassar, inspired, he wandered. Among the black macaques, the flapping hornbills, the wheeling *Ornithoptera* with satin yellow wings. From rotting jack-fruits, he scraped beetles for his collections. At the edges of the rugged territory of the Bugis, he watched rivers disappear into the earth. Brown snakes tangled in his net as he ruffled through the leaves impatiently, imagining what he could find for Darwin. It was summer. He sweated, bent his spectacles so they wouldn't slip from his nose.

Bug collector, species man. And yet now, in the patterns of the insects that he pushed pin by pin into his boxes, something greater had begun to reveal itself to him, though what it was he didn't know. He felt as he did when, walking through the jungle, he sensed the presence of another creature following in the understory, a presence that vanished when he turned to look. At night he began to dream of a generating machine, a clanking, screeching engine, in which old species were devoured, and from which new ones emerged, blinking, into the light.

Steadily he was making his way through the Archipelago, each hour ticking toward the night the angel would meet him on Ternate. Timor, Banda, Ambon. The islands among which he found himself in the early months of the year of his discovery were lush and forbidding, racked by earthquakes, or as he wrote: *tortured*. By now he was distracted by the immensity of his collections, mocked by their size and his inability to explain how such diversity had come to be:

Butterflies—620 species.
Moths—2,000 species.
Beetles—3,700 species.
Bees & Wasps—750 species.
Flies—660 species.
Bugs & Cicadas—500 species.
Locusts—160 species.
Dragonflies—110 species.

On the island of Gilolo, the forests bloomed with scarlet *Ixora*. In an abandoned Portuguese fort, he met a Dutch corporal and quartet of listless Malay soldiers, with krises rattling as they rose up from the stones. From a lean-to near the shore, he wandered into grasses that waved high above his head. He watched mound-builders bury their eggs on the shore, noted mimicry among orioles and honeysuckers, shot a ground thrush with azure shoulders. Shaking clots of insects from coconut blossoms, he joked to his assistant that God must hold a particular affection for the bees. His malaria returned. (*This fever,* he wrote, *this ague, familiar friend.*) Sick and miserable, he crossed the short channel to the island of Ternate, with its slumbering cone, where he sought to rest. Langsats and mangosteens ringed the town. In the ruins of the palace of the Sultan, he waited for his fever to break.

If his fame would one day become inextricable from Ternate, he knew it was but a coincidence, for it was in São Gabriel on the Rio Negro that he heard the river dwellers speak of shape-shifters; on Kalimantan, in the mildewed library of the White Rajah, that he read Ovid; and on Gilolo, in the high grass, fever massing as a storm, that he thought of Malthus and of death, and once he thought of death, he could not escape her, saw the trails limned with the carapaces of beetles, saw the strangling figs, saw rot, saw fragments of bone, shores of shattered coral, sea crabs, fish curled onto the sand. The solution—that it was death that eliminates the weakest, selects varieties, and thus shapes the forms fittest for survival—was so simple and so beautiful that the moment he uncovered it, it seemed impossible that he, or any man, could have believed anything else. He had been moving toward this moment. For months he had been moving. But it was on Ternate that the answer possessed him, sliding into him like a gun bolt, and he rose feverish from his bed, carrying the vision before him (and how he could feel it, that beautiful idea in all its completion, that warmth in the recesses of his eyes), carefully, delicately, as if it were an insect he did not wish to crush, and he sat and he began to write. *The life of wild animals is a struggle for existence . . .*

The whole field appeared in a single moment to Apelles, wrote Ficino, in another time and another place, *and aroused in him a desire to paint.* And so, pencil gripped against his tremors, the bug collector worked, wrapped in blankets when struck by chill, then stripped bare against the heat inside him. Epiphany or fever, he later did not know. The hours would blur, the sweat running in rivulets down his chest, his eyes burning with salt, his penis limp and damp on the cold slats of the rattan chair. There were moments when his whole body seemed to vanish, when he sensed the hovering of a ghost or angel, delivering inspiration from a world beyond his own. He was but a scribe. And when he awoke the following morning and found the essay complete, delivered to him by that other, it didn't occur to him to send it to anyone but Darwin.

He mailed it on March 9, 1858, in a packet of mail sent on a Dutch schooner bound for Java. His letter accompanying it was short, his words deferential. The essay was titled "On the Tendency of Varieties to Depart from the Original Type," and sought to explain the *extraordinary modifications of form, instincts, and habits* of the natural world. With luck the mail would be in Darwin's hands in ten weeks: mid-May. And Darwin would respond directly, as he had up until that day, his reply arriving in Ternate as early as July.

Letter steaming toward London, he felt a great emptiness. He planned to return to the forest, but in the days that followed, he haunted the shore, watched the horizon in expectation, as if somehow the idea could vault the seas. When he could bear the wait no longer, he set sail in the *Hester Helena* for New Guinea, hoping that the rhythm of collection would calm the running of his mind.

He landed at Dorey, on the northeast coast. The island was vast and mist-shrouded. He had wished to escape the unbearable joy of his discovery, fleeing as one might flee a desire from which there is no deliverance. But everywhere he looked he saw the struggle for existence. He could not happen upon an insect without wondering how every trait had saved it from nature's forge. Even the most delightful forms and colors were darkened by death's shadow. *This daily and hourly struggle,* he wrote in his journals. And again: *This incessant warfare.*

In the dim light of the Papuan forest, he found deerflies with horns beneath their eyes. He sucked the sweet wet air of mosses, identified the leeches that gathered on his ankles, hunted tree kangaroos and the elusive *Cuscus*. Wrapped in his reverie, he wandered without aim. He knew he was incautious, setting off into unfamiliar forests, now without assistants, unaware of the trail he followed and how he would return. But he heeded neither his good sense nor the imploring of his men. At night, back in his hut, they pulled snakes down from the rafters. Fever lit through his crew. Dysentery took away his boy Jumaat, whom they draped in white and buried in the sand.

In his second month, he fell and cut his ankle. The wound ulcerated; a local doctor's poultices only worsened the inflammation. For a month he couldn't leave his shelter. In his best moments he watched butterflies settle on the windowsill. He strained his eyes to identify them, but they were too far away to see. He imagined them new species, escaping, perhaps never to be caught again. In his worst moments, he clawed his leg in pain and screamed.

His only consolation was the thought of his letter, which by now had surely crossed the seas and arrived in London. He could see the envelope nestled in a mailbag, rustling against lovers' notes and gardeners' monthlies, moving steadily through the dark smoke of the city, the postman oblivious to the grace his bag contained. He imagined Darwin receiving it, alone. And alone, reading.

Boats passed in the distance: curled rafts that recalled to him the coracles of Welsh fishermen, and darting praus, and warships bristling with guns. It was August by the time another ship anchored off Dorey, to return him to Ternate. When he arrived there, he would have leapt to shore but for his ankle. Yes, said the harbormaster, looking up behind glasses empty of their lenses, there were packages awaiting him. But from Darwin: nothing. Yes, the man was certain, absolutely certain. Yes, for you, sir, I'll check again.

If his ankle still pained him, he no longer wrote of it. He was a man immune to solitude and yet now he felt alone as he never had before. In his mind, his beautiful idea paced, clenched and restless. To his housekeepers, a pair of Malay sisters, old girls with faces creased as deep as walnuts, he confessed the agony of waiting, led them through his collections, speaking of Natural Selection in a mixture of English and Bahasa Malay. They were good Mahometans, he wrote, and when he asked, *What made this plume, this armour? What made this lizard's skin?* they answered, *God is great,* to which he could agree, and *God is merciful,* which (thinking of the savagery of hummingbirds, his brother's fatal fever) he couldn't countenance. Each morning, he rose early and went to the dock to see if a ship had anchored during the night.

August passed.

These tortured islands. What had happened? By now, the response from Darwin should have arrived. Every day his worry deepened. Absentminded, he cut his palm prying mussels. The wind opened his unlatched shutters and spirited away his butterflies, his *Hestias,* his blues. Twice he upended the preserving arrack, until he was forced to buy from Chinese traders, who whispered that all Englishmen were drunks. There were, of course, infinite ways a letter could be lost, countless disasters that might befall a ship. But if so, he must act, and quickly. He could not risk waiting, lest the angel visit someone else. How many months had passed? He would—he must—write Darwin again.

And yet... And yet a faint voice urged restraint. For what if the letter *had* arrived at Down House? Crouching by the shore, he watched the fishermen. He had heard of no shipwreck, no pirates. And since July, he had received responses to all the other letters sent that same March day. Was Darwin ill? he wondered. If so, then he must wait. He must not seem overeager, lest his correspondent think him impudent. With the housekeepers of Ternate, he told himself, the secret was safe.

There was another possibility, of course, which he began to fear more with each passing day. It was not that his letter had been lost, but that it was, itself, to blame for the silence. This was it: he must have written lines of such offense or ignorance as to leave the great man no choice but to sever contact. Oh, why, he asked himself, had he not kept a copy of the letter or the essay? For as he tried to recall his words, they seemed to change, to metamorphose. Until they became so vile, so appalling, that he prayed there had been a shipwreck, dragging those pages beneath the sea.

Soon he was certain. Darwin, having read his note of

introduction, and finding it cordial, had turned to the accompanying essay, surprised perhaps that he had been sent a draft rather than a published piece, and yet graciously granting that his correspondent (and briefly he had to scan the letter to remember the name of the species man) was at the ends of the earth, without access to journals of the societies. But when he began to read, he found the ravings of a man in the fit of a fever. Bombastic, preposterous speculation was what it was, its logic victim to its author's ignorance, its thoughts so incomplete, so rushed, so absurd as to wreck all previous consideration that he had for this collector, who had dared initiate a correspondence when he, Darwin, had written just requesting ducks.

Yes: Darwin had dozens of such men as him; the rooms at Down House were filled with skins, with mollusks, ferns transported across the seas in great glass cases. He had been generous to consider the thoughts of such an ingénue. But there were limits to generosity. Who was Wallace, again? Could he remember him, haunting the Museum, in the same suit, day after day, smelling vaguely of a boarding-house, never wearing a school tie? Must he ask Lyell? For one cannot escape one's station. Hadn't Darwin written of a native, from Tierra del Fuego, raised in London, who had abandoned his English manners and returned to the barbarism of his race? *I could not have believed how wide was the difference between savage and civilized man: it is greater than between a wild and domesticated animal.* This from *The Voyage of the Beagle,* which the younger man had loved so much. Yes, he realized, it was only a matter of time before Darwin and the men of the academies would see him for what he was: a scavenger of windfall, the son of a bankrupt father, graceless in the parlour, nothing but a thin man with a net and the presumption that he belonged with them.

Bug collector, species man. But still beneath these fears, the dim embers of euphoria persisted, bursting forth at times in flames. No longer was it simply the vastness of life that moved him. No, now he looked upon the world, and what he saw was not life, but life transforming, sprouting sharper fangs and nectaries of ever sweeter nectar, taking flight as color danced kaleidoscopically across her wings. And all as nature culled the weakest, the slowest, the lesser-taloned: a force that had come rumbling toward this moment, and would rumble on, destroying its infinity of forms and bringing forth that many more.

His thumbs turned violet from the skins of mangosteens, and his journals turned violet from his thumbs. He no longer washed. Through the markets of Ternate he wandered, restless, racing each morning to check the mails. Did he wonder what he must look like to other men, possessed, a mind cargoed with a dream so beautiful that it had changed the very light that fell upon the world? No, he hadn't erred. He could no more doubt it than he could doubt every beetle, every sea star, every gilded hummingbird that he had collected on his journeys.

This was why Darwin could not respond. They too were working toward this solution, the good men of the Linnaean Society and the Royal Academy, and now this letter had come, postmarked from a village none had ever heard of, in the trembling hand of a young man half their age. *I have brought fire to their halls,* he wrote on pages stiff with dried arrack, and then obliterated the words. The months that had passed—the excruciating days of heat and waiting, the expectant gazing at the horizon, the incessant fantasies of opening a letter again and again—this was the time that it was taking to burn, for the flame to burst into a conflagration which would not stop until it destroyed everything, not only Genesis and Aristotle and Archbishop Ussher, but (and this he knew, for he knew the glory of the search) the very dream of Darwin himself.

If so, then he was waiting for the fire to find its tinder, for the Great Men to stand before the majesty of his discovery, to marvel. To marvel, and then, slowly, turning and staring out across their halls, to gather together and take it for their own. They knew (as did he) that such majesty did not befit a bug collector who had done his learning at the Mechanics Institute. He now understood why, earlier, Darwin had warned him, and so kindly. It was never his; it was his heresy to have ever thought so.

Then let it burn, he thought, stopping on the coralline shore, his pant legs rolled, the breakers stirring over his ankles. Let it burn and let the ashes settle. Its time had come. As Copernicus tore us from the universe's core, so let *them* be the ones to bear man these new tidings. Let *them* destroy Scripture and let *them* build from it a new world, this Gospel of deerflies and tree kangaroos. He would go back to the jungle. Let them have their fame; he cared only for wonder, and to wonder he would return.

In late September, with still no reply, he left for Gilolo. By then the letter from Down House was at sea, somewhere in the Indian Ocean, its words complimentary if careful, hinting nothing at the devastation the young collector had caused, the changes he had set in motion. But he could not know this, that autumn, in the forests of Gilolo, where he collected an unusual variety of lory, previously unknown to him, ornamented in red and blue and green, and then, a few days later, a day-flying moth, *Cocytia,* a species not only very beautiful, but extraordinarily rare.

FOR THE UNION DEAD

Last summer, in late July, I received a phone call from my father notifying me of the death of my Uncle Teddy, and asking me to come to San Francisco to help him sort through his brother's belongings before the movers came.

My uncle had no children. He had never married, and his girlfriend of many years had gone her own way for reasons—I would later learn—related to the story that will come. He was a quiet figure, my father's only brother, and very much overshadowed by my mother's sprawling clan of six siblings. Indeed, when I first heard of Teddy's death, I couldn't remember when I'd seen him last. By then, our weekend trips to San Francisco were very much a thing of the past. Even to this day, I can't recall the surname of that girlfriend, an apricot-hued woman who chain-smoked his Camels, and who, in contrast to my *Aunt* Deborah, my *Aunt* Judith, my *Uncle* Michael, et cetera, we all knew just as Donna. Nor did I remember any discussion of why they hadn't married, or why they had no kids. For me, it was just one of Teddy's particularities, like the Technicolor fuchsia of the borscht he drank each morning, or the elastic suspenders he wore over his off-white dress shirts, or the background drone of professional wrestling on his bedroom television, which seemed to cycle on some eternal loop.

In the beginning, it was the television that overcame my resistance to those long visits. At home, my mother had banished ours to the bedroom closet, to be watched only on special "movie nights," when it was hooked up to the VCR. But at some point, in one of the backroom negotiations I now know make up much of parenthood, my parents must have decided that TV at Teddy's was permitted. So, for a time, on a weekly basis, my sister and I would squeeze into the sofa chair of worn yellow corduroy that sat just inches from the screen. This was the age of the reign of Hulk Hogan and Randy "Macho Man" Savage and my uncle's favorite, André the Giant, who, he reminded me on several occasions, though French by birth, was Polish by extraction, and who I thought—for quite some time, and not without a degree of perplexity—was the same Andre as that in Malle's *My Dinner with Andre*, a film I often heard discussed among my parents and their friends. The television, a Sony Trinitron—half screen, half speaker—had twelve channels, accessed by a row of concave plastic buttons that gave off a satisfying *ping* when pressed. Still, I can't recall him watching anything but wrestling. Why this was, I never stopped to ask. Only later would I wonder whether there was something about the cartoon violence that served as a parody of all violence, and perhaps as a catharsis for the real kind that he'd seen.

For a living, my uncle ran a small convenience store on Geary, about a half mile from his apartment, purveying a mixture of American junk food and canned Eastern European imports to a motley group of Poles, Armenians, and Russians, alongside a smattering of patients and patients' families who wandered down from Mount Zion. I can still recall it, and from the height of someone no taller than my uncle's waist: the powdered Kool-Aid and Cadbury eggs beside the bonneted baby on the imported Alenka chocolates, the jars of hard candy in their squeaky cellophane, the storeroom with boxes—*boxes!*—of Topps wax packs. If we were lucky enough, my uncle would allow both of us to select a small toy or sweet, an act which, at that time, seemed to be less a demonstration of avuncular affection than evidence of untold wealth. Indeed, such was the stockroom bounty that it never even occurred to me that it was my father, a general practitioner with a growing private practice, who was more financially secure. I had grown up in an Eichler in the suburbs fifty miles south of the city, with a backyard spanned by two great redwoods that littered their feathered leaves across the insulation tarp on the small unheated pool. It was hardly great wealth—these were the pre-dot-com days, when a doctor could still buy a house in Silicon Valley—but we certainly had much more than Teddy, for whom financial planning consisted primarily of bribing his homesick Russian landlord with jars of pickled herring that he brined himself.

Like much else about my uncle, his differences from my father—differences, one could say, between the two Andres—might have simply been a product of their difference in age. Teddy was sixteen when my father was born in a Queens emergency room, a gap accounted for by six years of war, seven of statelessness, and two more of their mother's steadfast refusal to bring another child into a world that could take everything away. By the time my father arrived, the family's story—the flight, the work camps, the loss of a first son to Red Army conscription—was all part of a past not often spoken of. My father knew the map: Warsaw, Bialystok, the gulags outside of Archangelsk, then Tashkent, Kherson, Kiev, and back to Poland when the war was over. There, finding nothing, no one, they'd continued on to Paris, where they lived until they followed their sole surviving cousin to New York. By then Teddy spoke five languages, and none of them well. His vulgar Russian of the gulag nursery, his market Uzbek, his Ukrainian, his singsong French with pungent Belleville curses: they all served him primarily to play with other children. His Polish started to dissolve when, soon after they arrived in

Queens, my grandfather suddenly decreed the family would speak only "American," which remained for years a patois of pantomime and guessed-at words. Hence: the accent (*huishy-huashy, Daffy Dug*), the trouble with articles (absent in Uzbek, Russian, Polish), the seemingly random employ of gender-based possessive pronouns (absent in French). Even thirty years later, when I came to know Teddy, he still spoke tentatively. He was afraid, my father once told me, that others would think his imperfect English might suggest ingratitude. It was safer not to speak.

There was also their difference in physical appearance. My father was taller, stouter, his face tan from tennis and from our vacations. Teddy, who probably would have been tall if not for the childhood hunger, gave a fainter, paler impression, the hue, I would note with a shock one winter excursion to run our dog at Fort Funston, of driftwood, which, buffeted enough, grows grey and indistinct. Even in his forties, he wore black old-man slacks, their polyester polished to a sheen around the seat and knees. He walked with a limp, and though it was a limp from childhood—hip dysplasia, unrepaired, my father told me—it added to a sense of age. Even the apartment I arrived at that Sunday after Teddy passed away seemed to belong to someone of a prior generation. A short hallway gave onto a small dining room scarcely larger than the circular table at its center. Then clockwise: kitchen, living room, a second, tiny hallway leading to closet, bedroom, bath. The wall-to-wall carpeting was still the dirty buff of memory, as was the haphazard mix of "Turkish" rugs. The walls were empty but for a mounted set of commemorative plates from the U.S. Bicentennial, and some scattered oils—a horn of plenty, a mountain sunset—purchased over the years at flea markets and neighborhood sales.

On my father's suggestion, we began in the living room. The old brown couch would go, of course, as would the dark credenza, pine stained to look like chestnut, filled mostly with issues of *Time* dating from the eighties. There were some old Sears catalogues, and shoeboxes organized on unclear principles: paperweights bedded with watch parts, and keys to far more houses, cars, and lockboxes than my uncle could have possessed. I was aware then of the difference between what I saw and what my father was seeing. I was struck mostly by the anonymity of the objects, their forlornness; he lingered over them. Yet when I wondered aloud if there was a story behind any of the artifacts, my father shook his head. It was striking, he told me, how little reminded him of his brother—indeed, how little of the apartment reflected his brother's inner life at all. Unless of course one reflected that one feature of that inner life was to keep itself hidden. Rather, he was thinking—he said—what he'd been thinking for days, namely how much he regretted that he had not pressed Teddy to accept more of his charity. I probably didn't know, he told me, but it had been his brother who had supported him during medical school, had moved with him to the Bay Area; it was only fair to pay him back. But Teddy always refused. While at first my father attributed such stubbornness to personal dignity, over time, as the two of them began to separate in station, he'd come to understand it differently. Teddy never seemed to begrudge my father's success. He was drunk and expansive at my parents' wedding, laughing even at the inside jokes he didn't understand. He gave a wedding gift, a set of crystal glasses from Neiman Marcus, completely inconsistent with his tastes and far too generous. When I was born, and long before I was walking, he gave me a bicycle, just as he bought ballet slippers for my sister, as if to stake a claim on milestones to come.

Over time, my father said, he'd come to wonder if such extravagance was Teddy's recognition of the diverging paths their lives would take, something he recognized long before my father. And indeed it happened, my father increasingly in the clinic, or attending an art house film series with friends, or taking us on summer camping trips. Trips to which, he added, he frequently invited his brother and Donna, knowing full well they would refuse. What the Malle film was to "The Giant," Arches National Park was to Reno, where Donna gambled and my uncle, I assume, must have spent his time doing something other than eating, and yet the only photos showed him (dressed in that off-white dress shirt, arm slung over Donna's shoulder) against the bounty of the buffets.

They were an odd couple. Now I suspect he was drawn to her for the sheer volume of her Americanness—for her big American hair and bright white patent leather heels, for the brooches, bracelets, earrings that jingled out her presence well before she entered a room. Even her bust, hammocked in pink and chartreuse polyester blouses, seemed somehow American in the brash way it called attention to its size. She was of stone fruit farming stock; the family went as far back as anyone could go in Santa Clara County, she said, "without being Miwoks." She had a history of epilepsy, and though it had been decades since she'd had a seizure, she had never learned to drive, and so my uncle chaperoned her everywhere. For as long as I knew him, he drove a Pontiac Bonneville, a model from the early seventies that reminded my sister and me of the cars driven by kidnappers in the ominous school educational videos that taught us not to talk to strangers. For Donna's part, it was hard to say what, apart from the chaperoning, she saw in my uncle. He was handsome, or at least seemed to once have been handsome, and I can recall the occasional waitress, check-out girl, or, later, nurse who was quite charmed by his courtly manners or his accent. But Donna showed almost no interest in where he'd come from. She hated the herring and the borscht, and not once did I hear her ask him about Europe. Indeed, she seemed to have almost no awareness of Teddy's story at all. My father didn't know whether this was because his brother didn't want to tell her or because she didn't want to know; his guess was both, which might go some way toward explaining their compatibility. Or maybe it was this, he said: for him she was uncommon, and we all want to be uncommon, and the moment she realized the error of her understanding was the moment that she left.

Anyway, my father continued, he now regretted the distance that had grown between them, particularly as time went on, and my sister and I grew older, and our weekends filled with sports and friends. They still spoke, but then my father got an affiliated position at the university and began to teach and travel more, and sometimes weeks would pass before he saw his brother. It was because of this, he said, that he wasn't really certain how my uncle began to develop his interest in the war—the Civil War, he added—save that it had begun with Donna. At the time, he didn't think it was remarkable. He had seen his brother go through a similar period of interest in his adopted country at the time of the Bicentennial, though this had a seeking, sad quality to it, as if the commemorative plates, the flag placed on his balcony, were ways of trying out an identity he didn't possess. My father could remember how on that Fourth of July he and my mother had gone with Teddy and Donna to watch the celebrations. Parades were not something my father went to regularly—they were, he liked to say, only for children or for fascists. But Teddy was different. He never spoke of the connection between his observance of certain holidays—the Fourth, Memorial

Day, Veterans Day—and the fact that, due to his hip, he had been turned down when he tried to enlist. My father was of course a baby at the time of those deferrals, but in later years, he sensed that the sole thing his brother ever envied him for was his service as a physician in the Navy during Vietnam. Indeed, much of his brother's patriotism stemmed, he thought, not from pride, nor even gratitude, but rather from a kind of longing. After all, he told me, even though his parents never returned to Poland, they still had a home in memory to carry with them. Teddy, meanwhile, found himself in the impossible position of missing something he'd never possessed.

But yes, the Bicentennial: for all my father's suspicion of patriotism, it began auspiciously. The mood was festive. The slopes of Golden Gate Park were blanketed with drumming corps, students dressed as redcoats played war among the eucalyptuses, and beauties with long white gloves waved from convertibles bedecked with paper flowers. Donna was dressed in skintight striped red pants and a starry bodice. She'd purchased paper tricornes from a vendor, for my parents and for Teddy, who placed his at a jaunty angle over thinning hair. He seemed utterly enraptured by the pageantry, said my father, by the parades, the high school bands and floats. It was only later in the day, when my father was returning from the restroom, that he happened to see his brother at a moment when Teddy thought no one was looking, standing in the middle of the cheering crowd with a look of such disconsolation, such unmooring, that my father felt he was for the first time seeing his brother as he really was.

And so when, ten years later, Donna announced that she and Teddy planned to visit historic sites in Gettysburg and Philadelphia, my father recalled that vision of his brother at the Bicentennial, and couldn't help but wonder if they should travel somewhere else. But he couldn't explain why, and in any case Donna's sister had gone and said it was incredible, really, and they had already bought the tickets. As it turned out, Teddy, on his return, said almost nothing about the trip. He did not seem anguished, nor particularly thrilled. Were it not for the little Liberty Bell replicas he bought for me and my sister, it almost seemed as if he hadn't even been there at all. All of which explained the surprise my father felt when, some months later, he called the shop and Donna told him that my uncle had flown east again, this time for a guided bus tour of famous battle-grounds in seven states.

"Apparently, it's his new hobby," she said.

My father remained at the phone for some time after she hung up. He didn't know what to think, he told me. It seemed out of character; indeed, there was something even humorous about the image of his brother, in his dress shirts and suspenders, following a group of heartland tourists with their ball caps and their cameras slung about their necks. But then, not three months after his return,

Teddy was on another flight, this time to Georgia. Soon my father found Teddy's dining table stacked with volumes from the Inner Sunset library: books on famous battles, biographies of Grant and Sherman, guides to uniforms and arms. *Particularly* guides to uniforms, he told me, which should have been his clue, for it was around this time that the reenactments began.

He asked me whether I remembered these, and I answered that I did. Like much about my uncle, I hadn't thought of it in years, but now that it was mentioned, I could still recall the day my sister discovered the vintage revolver in Teddy's bedroom closet, and the subsequent explanation that my uncle offered to my enraged mother. At the time, the gun had clearly overshadowed all other aspects of the story, though in retrospect, it seems amazing that I didn't find it at least a little odd that my uncle—who still substituted the French *mais* for the English *but,* and still called Rice Krispies *kasha* and most fruits by their Uzbek names (for it was in Tashkent, at the age of ten, that he ate his first peach, first plum, first orange)—had found such purpose in dressing up with a group of strangers, to act out the battles that had burned across fields and pastures so far from his life. But I was eleven when the reenactments started, and still at the age when most adults were equally intriguing and dull. Teddy's possession of a grimy Union uniform, or the image of him charging across a field with other reenactors, was about as remarkable as my Uncle

Steven's double joints, or the huge plastic trophies my Aunt Deborah had collected in her softball league, enough to cover a whole wall.

I told my father this.

He nodded. And yet the funny thing, he said, was that at the time, as far as hobbies went, *he* hadn't found it terribly strange. It was certainly more interesting than "Wrestling Mania" or whatever those ridiculous orgies called themselves. And this was the time of *Glory* and the Ken Burns film. He found his patients reading bookmarked copies of *Battle Cry of Freedom* in the waiting room; he himself was slowly making his way through Shelby Foote. A few years later, a reenactment of the Battle of Gettysburg would draw some *tens* of thousands of participants. The papers and TV loved to cover the events, the tone of the reporting sometimes whimsical, sometimes a bit condescending, but usually ending with a kind of elegiac hopefulness that the battles could serve as some kind of ritual in which scars both new and distant might be healed. Nor was he the only one to see how the reenactment of some kind of imaginary Civil War might offer a kind of baptism for those whose families had come from somewhere else. Indeed, even years later, he could recall a television program that had featured extensive interviews with both an expat who traveled each year from Stockholm to don the grey outfit of a Confederate soldier, and a Rhode Islander of Japanese extraction who was "serving" in a Union regiment. Both men, my father said, had testified that participation in the reenactments had for the first time in their lives made them feel truly American, though whether or not this was true for Teddy my father didn't know. In any case, he said, he never exactly understood *what* it was that Teddy did at the reenactments until a conversation he had with Donna, at the beginning of the end of Teddy's life.

It was early August. By then Teddy had spent over a decade making almost yearly visits to the battlefields, beginning at Bull Run in 1993 and ending that July, at the Battle of the Crater, when, the day after the reenactment, as he was waiting in the airport lounge of Richmond International, a blood clot, which had likely formed as he lay on the battleground, broke free from the deep veins of his calf. And then, on the CT scan at Bon Secours St. Mary's Hospital: not only the pulmonary embolism, but the lung cancer, already the size of his fist.

Against the doctor's advice, Teddy flew home to San Francisco for the surgery, which was where, in the waiting room, Donna, who remained a friend despite their separation and her subsequent marriage, told my father about the singular nature of his brother's devotion. My father could still recall the afternoon, the room with its samovars of lukewarm coffee, the children cavorting over the laps of anxious parents, the flickering monitor with the first three letters of each patient's name. It was, he said, the longest conversation he had had with her, and it was deeply moving to feel the intimacy that formed around the possibility of loss. Interestingly, she had assumed that his brother had told him much more about his forays. When he corrected her, she told him Teddy was probably just waiting for him to ask.

She paused, and after some consideration said, "You know he just went to die, right?"

My father, who had glanced up at the progress screen, thought for a moment that in his worry, he had missed something. "I'm sorry?"

"To die," she said. "In battle."

But still he didn't completely understand. Didn't most of them "die"? he asked.

"*Eventually,*" she said. "But Teddy never even fought."

She clarified: moments after the bugler opened the re-enactment, my uncle would just walk toward the fighting and lie down.

"Just?"

"Just."

"Really?"

Were his brother not on the operating table, my father told me, he might have laughed in disbelief.

"Really," Donna said.

Teddy never made it to the surrender, never stayed for the fairs and dances and trivia nights that followed. Never drank with the other soldiers, neither the "authentic" whiskey from the shared flasks, nor the anachronistic beers that occasionally appeared in anachronistic coolers as if from outer space. Not only that, but my father also had to understand the context, Donna told him. For if anything unites the reenactors, it is the desire to remain alive as long as possible, to participate in the history that they have prepared for so meticulously. Indeed, she said, it was a common complaint among the organizers (not to mention an apparent object of ridicule among the spectators) that none of the grown men playing soldiers wanted to die, and particularly not so early on. Who would? And miss the festivities, lying amongst the cow patties, while all around you, your comrades charged into history with rifles gleaming? Even when a bullet's strike was undeniable, said Donna, most men would feign an injury, calling for comrades to transport them to the medical tent and the attentions of the nursing volunteers. But not his brother. Not Teddy, who spent untold amounts of his dwindling savings on ever more authentic uniforms, not to mention plane flights and car rentals, and "event rates" charged by roach motels. Not Teddy, who stood on shivering mornings at Vicksburg and Spotsylvania, at Shiloh and Chickamauga, as around him thousands of fellow soldiers, guns stuffed with paper cartridges, shifted beneath their heavy packs. Not Teddy, who—when the clarion broke across the pastures, at Seven Pines and Opequon, and the smoke bombs began to fly at Franklin and Fort Stedman—lay down on the mossy forest path, or beside the bursting blooms of buttonbush, or in the fields. Always on his back and looking up, said Donna, who one afternoon, watching at Antietam, realized that, as much as she loved this man, there was a part of him that would always remain far beyond her reach. Just as she understood that she would leave him, not out of animosity and not with bitterness—for life at seventy-five was too short for either—but because what he was seeking was something she couldn't provide.

He would lie there for hours in that strange vigil, as around him the fighting raged, and slowly, reluctantly, one by one, the others began to fall, sprawling with cries or dramatic gurgles, tearing at hidden bladders of red coloring, tumbling theatrically from their mounts. Sometimes far away, or sometimes near him, sometimes even touching, resting a hand or head upon his chest. And as the pastures filled, he remained unmoving, the warm sun on his face, or the cold of the winter soil of Fredericksburg seeping through his coat, his back, his aching hip. Until at last the bugler sounded and, all at once, together, the dead rose from the consecrated, hallowed ground.

By then it was late afternoon, and an unexpected sun had broken through the summer fog that rolled unimpeded up and down San Francisco's long western flank. From the living room, we moved on to a little workroom my uncle had set up in a hallway closet, with mason jars of nuts and bolts, and sundry pieces of wood gathered in the blue

Danish sugar cookie tins, where one day they could be found if needed. Then the kitchen, the refrigerator empty save for a tub of sour cream and a two-liter bottle of kvass. We would leave this. Just as we would leave the simvastatin and the digitalis in the bathroom, the dress shoes with their replacement shoelaces, the pantry stocked with jars of cat food he used to mix with sugar and leave out for strays.

In the bedroom, a heating pad still warmed the sofa chair; the paramedics must have left it on. The chair would go, as would the flanking oxygen stand and vaporizer, and the Trinitron with the push-button channels: the Trinitron to which, one March, Teddy hooked up a VCR he'd borrowed from my parents, to play for me an episode of WrestleMania he'd purchased specially by mail order. My parents had gone out to dinner, and so we watched the full three hours, fight after fight, culminating in the moment when—to quote the jubilant words of the announcer—"The Irresistible Force met The Immovable Object," and Hulk Hogan lifted André, trembling and helpless as Antaeus, and brought him thundering down.

The photographs were in the closet, its mirrored door now bearing a long, diagonal crack. He had kept them in a series of old wooden cigar boxes, next to the Union outfits. I suspect my father had known that we would find them there, and that he had waited because he knew that after he found them, he wouldn't go on. The room was dark, the only window gave onto the apartment parking lot, where a couple was yelling at each other in Russian, and so we brought the photos into the living room and laid the boxes on the table before the couch. We were all there—Donna with her flowered polyester blouses, and my sister with her braces, and my uncle sitting beside me at an ice-cream parlor on a day that suddenly returned to me with such vividness that I could taste (and as I write, can still taste) the cold ribbons of caramel in the melting cream. There was a pair of early photos of my grandparents, taken in a Warsaw studio, and others, of my parents' wedding, of Thanksgivings and Bar Mitzvahs and high school graduations that I hadn't remembered Teddy attending. And then, at last, the photos of the war—not the one he had survived, but the one that, repeatedly, he didn't. In contrast to the snapshots, these were different: large-format commemorative photographs of the reenactments, in period sepia or black-and-white, the scenes instantly, utterly familiar from the albumen prints of Mathew Brady, with their field tents and broken ramparts, their scattered cannons and bodies strewn across the field. And on every photo: a tiny arrow, etched in careful blue ballpoint, which showed, among the countless fallen soldiers, which one he was.

THE SECOND DOCTOR SERVICE

Sirs—Having read with interest Dr. Bennett's recent report of the young woman with episodic amnesia and transformation of personality, as well as Dr. Slayer's study "On the So-called Cumberland Were-wolf," I have spent the past months in deliberation over whether to share my own case with your readers. If I have hesitated, it is less out of concern for privacy than the simple fact that, though bearing the title of physician, I am but a country doctor, whose medical expertise extends little beyond those afflictions befalling the farmers and milk-maids of K— County. Indeed, it is likely that I never would have opened your learned *Journal* were it not for the very strange events that have befallen me this past year. Most of the members of your Society, I am aware, publish with that noble aim of advancing medicine; I write with the hope that one of them has encountered a case similar to my own, and so might save me before it is too late.

Unlike with most illnesses, Sirs—which arise within us insidiously, creeping through vein and fiber, unsettling our slumber, gradually awakening within us that ineffable, horrific sense of *dis-ease*—it is possible to state the very *instant,* indeed the very *longitude and latitude,* of my affliction, being four strokes after Twelve Noon on August 24, 1882, on the cusp of Mersey's Ridge, outside of S—. I was returning from a sick call; the patient was a parson's son who had fallen ill with a tertian fever. I had attended to him for three days and nights with the constant application of Beedham's Ointment and, upon restoring him to health, had saddled my horse and begun my journey home. It was a warm summer day, one of those particularly gilded morrows when the air swarms with motes of pollen, and the scent of wet grass rises from the fields, and everywhere life appears to swirl in such a miasma that I have wondered since if I did not inhale some invisible animalcule as I galloped up the hill, and that it is perhaps upon this beastie that I should lay the blame for all that followed. Down in the valley, the noon bells had tolled thrice when there arose a very strong odor of chestnuts, overwhelming the sweet scent of the grass and the sharp bloom of all the goldenrod stirred up by my horse's feet. This was impossible, of course: chestnuts would not be in season until November, and this thought, delivered whole and instantaneously between the third and fourth tolling of the bells, seemed to carry on its wings the conviction that something odd and terrible was to occur. It was then, just as I crested the hill, expecting the spectacular vision of the forests below, that I found myself not before that view, but somehow *five miles farther,* thundering over the bridge at Wilson's Mill.

We are all accustomed, I believe, to the experience of traveling and drifting into distraction, only to arrive safely at our destination as if directed by some unseen hand. My first suspicion was that this was what had happened, and yet I also knew it wasn't so: I had passed along this road a thousand times, and not once had I failed to stop on its descent into that ancient forest of beech and linden, where the soft light filters down through the whispering leaves, and the air is filled with the gay tintinnabulation of the chickadees, and the odor of the mushrooms and mosses never fails to awaken in me a profound nostalgia for my childhood adventures amidst those cathedrals of fallen boughs. Nor, I knew, could I have fallen asleep, for the road is too perilous, with hanging limbs that can dispatch even the most alert traveler. Such is my reasoning in retrospect; at the time it was a particular *sensation* that told me something was different, a feeling, unlike any other I had experienced, of *complete nothingness,* as if an *ellipsis* had occurred between the fields of goldenrod on Mersey's Ridge and the linden depths of the Mill, as if time and distance had somehow *folded* upon themselves, or—to put it differently—as if I had simply ceased to be.

There is little more to be said about this incident, save that it was the first. Shaken, I continued my ride. I stopped at H— to dine, finding myself in the company of an old friend. I made no mention of the event, ate heartily, and, having steadied my nerves, continued home.

For the next two months, nothing happened. I entered my forty-eighth year in the finest of health, save an old toothache and the gout in my right knee. The oaks autumned, followed by the beeches; the parson's boy fell sick again; I rode back and forth over Mersey's Ridge without an incident. In October, I was invited to a Ball in H—, to raise funds for the Deaf School there. Now, since my youth I have dreaded such decorous affairs, preferring the simpler company of my patients. But the School was dear to Constance, my wife, who has devoted many of her hours to helping those unfortunates. And so it was that I traveled with her to that town, where, in the gaily lit ballroom, I suffered the second of my paroxysms.

Again, I can time the exact moment of the seizure. I was standing in a crowd of doctors and doctors' wives, enduring the rambling braggadocio of a Mission Surgeon who had recently returned from curing Surinam of her hydroceles. He was attempting to shock the ladies, speaking ominously of natives who carted their tuberous scrota about in wheelbarrows, when I noted that same odor of chestnuts and, glancing at the clock, *observed it to advance in one clean stroke* from 7:15 to 7:48. Perplexed, I raised my wineglass to my mouth, only to find it empty. Around me the others, nearly a dozen in number, were watching me, laughing. I was certain I had gaffed. Nervously I looked about the circle, and yet the laughter was welcoming, as if the crowd were eagerly anticipating more. Fortunately, someone rang a bell. Dancing would begin! I turned to Constance, expecting to be scolded. Instead, with a little laugh, a toss of her frizzed bangs, and breath that lifted her bosom against her pale blue bodice, she uttered those words that would prove fatally prescient— *Whatever, Service, has come into you?* Then, with a pleased shiver of the silken rump of her skirts, she led me to the floor.

Of course, I still had no idea what had happened. Dizzied by the absurd notion that I was absent from a conversation in which I had so clearly taken part, I tried to pry the story from Constance as we waltzed. She was happy to rehearse the episode—apparently I had given the braggart surgeon quite a humbling, and in such a subtle manner that he had scarcely realized what was happening until it was too late. *Myself,* I thought, humbling *him*! However I might have wished to do such a thing, I don't think I have humbled anyone in my life. The waltz ended, a mazurka started up; though my knee ached, I joined her again if only to collect my thoughts. Of course I immediately associated the attack with the strange occurrence at Mersey's Ridge, for both the sweet aroma that preceded it and that identical sense of a profound, impenetrable void. Clearly, I thought, as the circle turned, I had suffered a *fit,* an *ecstasy,* an *alienation* from my mental faculties. And yet as to the source of this delirium, I remained utterly in the dark. It had neither the wildness of *mania transitoria,* nor the residual symptoms that tend to sift in the wake of an *apoplexy,* nor the violence that accompanies *lycanthropy* and those other perverse transformations of the soul. The premonition of chestnuts, the suddenness of onset, the total lapse of consciousness followed by my precipitous, if slightly stunned, return—all, of course, pointed to epilepsy, if not the *grand mal* of fame, the *larval* or *petit* form, known sometimes simply as the *absence.* But, while not an expert on the nerves, I have attended, twice, to patients diagnosed with this affliction, and while both reported a similar sense of vanishing during their attacks, both *appeared* vacant before the world, whereas I, apparently, *appeared* to have been possessed by none other than myself.

If I had regarded my first attack with some nonchalance, I found that the second left me with a severe disquiet. Like the tertian of the parson's son, my affliction had declared itself as a form prone to repeat. And while two months separated the first and second attacks, it was but a fortnight before it returned a third time, while I was hunting with my brother Thomas, who'd come from Boston on a visit. Again the attack was heralded by the smell of chestnuts, again the onset was sudden, again the amnesia total. We had spread a blanket out for supper. The dogs lay resting at my feet. I looked up at the sky and saw a distant nimbus, thought, *It will rain,* and then—as if I had summoned the clouds myself—I was on my mount, riding, a heavy rill streaming from the brim of my hat and onto a clutch of four wet quail, their black-grey feathers ruffling with the wind.

I screamed. I could not hold it back. So sudden was the change, so grotesque the bloodied birds! I pulled up my horse. I dismounted. Rain tickled down my collar. I felt a horrid sensation, as if something were fleeing me, some kind of vermin scurrying across my skin. I tore off my coat, my scarf, opened my shirt.

It was then that I caught my brother's eye. Thomas removed his hat, and wiped his sleeve across his forehead. *Richard?* he said. The dogs, too, I saw, were watching, with their own puzzled, canine airs.

Embarrassed, I muttered something, tried to climb back on my horse, slipped and fell into the mud. Thomas dismounted, to de-bog me. Are you ill? he asked.

I shook my head. A swoon, I said. Only nerves! Don't worry, *I am not myself*—that's all.

It was this phrase that did it. A common enough turn, of course: never do we stop to think exactly what it means. But with these words, the slumbering fears that had been with me since my first attack came pouring out. I stuttered out a confession. Thomas listened. He tried to comfort me, denied perceiving any change at all. We'd had a normal lunch, argued heartily about the Wool Tax Repeal, packed our bags, and resumed hunting. Indeed, if there had been any difference, he added with a laugh that was meant to comfort me, *it was for the better.* I even seemed without my typical brooding. A *seizure*? No. He wasn't a medical man, but he'd known many afflicted with seizures. They were all *tumbling fellows,* certainly none had carried on as I did, none had such opinions on the Revenue Code, none—and here he indicated the birds—were such fine shots.

A fine shot! Sirs, I have, in my life, never been "a fine shot." Whether it is a mild tremor, or a fondness for Nature's gentler creatures, something always seems to unsteady my hand when I attempt to pull the trigger. I go hunting for love of the out-of-doors, for the manly company, for the beneficial effects of fresh air on the lungs. If I have returned with bounty, it is only out of the pure chance crash of ball and prey. Thus while four quail in a single afternoon might have been welcomed by most, for me it came as a terrifying aberration. I was *not* myself; something *had* come into me, and if no change was observed in my countenance, this was not proof of the intruder's clemency, but rather the sophistication of his deception. By then I had spent enough time in our County Association Library in search of insight into my condition to know about the violence man commits in altered states. I speak of the district-court judge who, seizing, would rise at his supper and, with the clatter of silverware trailing in his wake, commence such a devastation that his family had no choice but to employ a strongman to wrestle him into submission. Or the case reported by Hoyle of the somnambulist who awoke to find himself dining on raw meat from the icebox. Or the virtuous young lady of Northampton who, in fits of insanity, would seek congress with chimney sweeps and rag mongers. Or the young schoolteacher-turned-murderer who, following his execution, was found to have a massive tumor of the temporal lobe. Or Pritchard's epileptic, who woke with magpies in his pockets and *with no such memory of what had occurred.*

Can you imagine, Sirs, what it is like to pass one's hours like this, waiting, knowing that at any moment you will be transformed? That you could retire to the sitting room, only to find yourself standing among the shards of your treasured china, blood on your hands, some leering ragman on your flanks? I feared each new smell, each puff of wind. The seizures were massing, I knew. As if I were some kind of monstrous human Leyden jar, the current gathering force until it was ready to discharge. And discharge it did, with ever increasing frequency. At dinner, I lifted a piece of ham to my mouth only to find myself swallowing pudding. I tossed my grandson in the air, and caught my dimpled, giggling granddaughter. I began Genesis 25 and finished Exodus 11. I unsheathed the knife I used for my Caesarians and found myself with a bonneted baby in my arms. But no matter how complete the *alienation,* there was no crime, no *morbid* transformation. When I inspected the surgical sites repaired by my Imposter, there was not a stitch awry. By every account, I was very much the same man. Indeed, Constance confirmed what my brother had noted: this second Dr. Service was perhaps a subtle *improvement* on the first. *He* didn't lick his comb. *He* didn't swear, *he* didn't clean *his* nostrils by advancing his handkerchief into them; when he spit, it was done in small volumes, with good aim, and without noisy preamble. He was even—I learned after a seizure struck while I was being photographed at the annual meeting of the County Association—ever so slightly handsomer: less stooped, with a "twinkle" in the eye and a smile befitting the confidence of a man who hides a secret from the world. As to the nature of this secret, I could only wonder. It wasn't long, however, before I suspected its relation to a new flush in Constance's cheeks, a new limpid depth to her gaze—a suspicion, Sirs, which filled my heart with man's most ancient envy, an envy unmitigated by the realization that the cuckold and the cuckoo were the same.

Let me return, though, to the County Association photograph. How many hours I spent staring at it! I don't know what, exactly, I was seeking, save that somewhere in his visage I expected to find an explanation of who he...I...*we*...were. He wore *my* black overcoat and *my* top hat and *my* silken grey ascot, which Constance had given me for *my* birthday. His mustache was waxed into the sharpest arabesque (mine was in the "natural" style). While the velvet collar of *my* overcoat had a tendency to accumulate all forms of detritus, his was finely brushed; the satin of the hat almost glistened. But it was into the eyes that I found myself staring. The more I studied them, the more I perceived, beyond their gay façade, something more profound, a perplexity and quiet sadness that one often encounters in the eyes of those who have struggled with the mysteries of the world. Indeed, the more I considered it, the more I came to think that however strange this *possession* had been for me, it must have been so much stranger for him. A babe, you will admit, is spared the horror of its birth by virtue of its stupidity. It need not ask where it comes from, or whether the sun will rise tomorrow, or what will become of its soul when the worms descend upon its flesh. And yet the second Dr. Service was forced to take up the very reins of life that morning of his awakening on Mersey's Ridge. Was he born, then, knowing how to ride? If so, are we all conceived with perfect capabilities? Is what man calls Learning actually a winnowing of innate wisdom? Is it the newborn who is the true sage, while the wise old man is but an illusion of sagacity, perpetrated by his whiskers and his cane?

Or perhaps he hadn't been so perfectly conceived. Had he come from elsewhere? Was this less a possession than a collision, a stone skipping across a pond, an errant soul in transmigration, who had the misfortune of landing not in a newborn but a man of forty-eight, with his melancholies and his gouty knees?

Or was he I, divided? A cutting which, cleaved from the stock, goes on to send forth its own roots? Or the corybantic twitching of a severed lizard's tail, which eventually grows still? Were my memories his? What happens, Sirs, to the soul of the sea cucumber when the sea cucumber is cut in two?

The more I pondered my condition, the more such questions gave onto others, budded, and bred, until they churned with such violence inside my mind that I had to do something to set them free. But to whom was I to turn? When I dared speak of my illness to Constance, she could scarcely hide her irritation. By then, she too had been transformed, into a raven-eyed Messalina who endured her *first* husband as if *he*—I!—were the aberration. My brother was in Boston. I dared not approach another physician lest he commit me to an asylum against my will.

This left only my double. I contrived, therefore, to seek him out directly, tucking about my person various inquiries, in the hope that during my paroxysms, he might place his hand into my coat pocket, discover one of the missives, and in turn reply regarding who he was, and where he had come from, and—and this I added only with hesitation—*what he would become.* Constance, driven to fury by the scraps that made their way into her possession, begged me to stop. So I had experienced a change, she said: What of it? Such is the way of life; we are never the same people we once were. Enough! she pleaded. Think what would happen if the authorities discover you! You will lose your patients, your practice, your... *our*... home.

But by then I didn't care. By then, with winter drawing on, I'd experienced, for the first time, two seizures in the course of a single day. I *needed* to reach him, if only to strike some kind of entente. I begged, I reasoned, my thoughts bubbled to my lips. I reminded him that it was I who gave him life. I haggled, offering him all he wanted if he would only swear to continue granting my return. I warned him of the fate of the parasite that mistakenly destroys its host.

Nothing. No reply. No word of comfort. No tear-stains of fellow suffering on my lines of ink. Everywhere, I found myself surrounded by the creeping evidence of his passage: the fingerprints on the crystal Constance told me to reserve for visitors, the tooth marks on my pipe stem, those humid sheets. But still he remained deaf to my entreaties. Deaf, Sirs—and then one evening in December, on the top shelf of my library, a sheath of papers caught my gaze. I can still recall my trembling hands as I climbed the bookcase ladder, certain I had found that long-awaited letter from my other half. And yet, as I brought the pages into the light, I found to my surprise what appeared to be a novel. It was unfinished, with corrections scattered over the manuscript, and if not the confession I'd hoped for, it was proof, nonetheless, that "R. Servus, Or: the Slave," as the author called himself, did not live a life of naïve indifference, but grappled, as I did, with the puzzling mystery of his transformation.

It was a long work—I do not have time to set down all the details here. I will distill it to the following: a young nobleman named Gaspard, after years of dissolution, meets, like Goethe, his double riding down a wintry path. But while the German's famous vision vanished as soon as it appeared, the protagonist of Servus's tale rides for a while *with* his doppelgänger, the latter telling him the story of the life he led up to the moment of their meeting. The second Gaspard's story is oddly similar to the first, if a bit lustier, culminating in the night when he (the second Gaspard), returning from his mistress's castle, meets *his* double on a mountain road. We are then treated to what seems to be the story of a third Gaspard, except this time familiar details begin to suggest themselves, and with a chill, we realize, as the first Gaspard does, that he is being told the story of his own life, through that same wintry night when he meets his double on the road. And as the second Gaspard continues to speak, the first Gaspard begins to feel a terror growing in his heart, a remembrance that the vision of one's double is said to be an omen of impending death. At that moment, *driven by a force not his own,* he reaches into his cloak and finds a dagger—a black dagger with a ruby in its hilt—a dagger he never owned!—leaps from his horse and—

But as I turned the page, I found only blank paper. I turned back, suspecting the final page had adhered to its predecessor, but there was nothing. Frantic then, I redoubled my search, extracting volume after volume from my shelves, finding nothing other than those scraps that bore my own pathetic queries. It was nearly dawn. I began to feel ill—my head ached—I knew with certainty that the fate of Gaspard held the secret to my own. The violence of the novel, that last, terrifying image of the strange dagger, could not but foretell a bloody finale. Surely, I thought, the first Gaspard would kill the second! But then what? Would he find himself exorcised of the demon? Or, the moment he plunged the blade into the Other's heart, would he feel its cold steel enter his own? What fantasy did my shadow live out on these pages? Was this a fear? A threat? Until that day I thought him indifferent to my existence, and if not indifferent, at the very least curious, maybe grateful, maybe even sorry for the man from whose head, Athena-like, he'd sprung. Now I knew it wasn't so. This was why the squatter had never answered my entreaties. He *wished* me to go mad! To lose my mind so that *he* might gain it. I was his enemy, his rotting limb, *his* parasite, the dying master of the kingdom he would one day rule.

By then, Constance was knocking at my door. I gathered up the scattered pages. She couldn't know! There was no hope in trying to explain—she would never believe—she would insist I wrote it. No, it was more insidious: *she already knew.* That was it, I realized, with horror: she *knew,* she was *waiting* for me to go, so as to welcome that usurper completely to her bed. I smelled chestnuts—I leapt up to hide the volume—*he, they* couldn't know I'd found it—I gained the ladder—I felt a wind—I cried out briefly—and then his tongue choked back my own.

I awoke in our carriage, gliding across the winter fields. Constance was sleeping, and for the longest time, I knew not where we were.

And so I find myself. Sirs, if I write to you now with some composure, if my pen is steady, if my words measured—Sirs, if this seems so, you must trust me when I say that it was but weeks ago that you would not have recognized me for the wild frenzy with which I fought my fate. Oh, I was like the drowning man who, gasping, bursts from placid waters, only to be pulled back in. Every ounce of my force was devoted to *his* destruction. (There were three of us then: Servus and I, and the terror that drove me to destroy him.) I didn't sleep—no: slumber I would leave for He-I-Hatched. I paced, I muttered, ranted, raced my mare into the fiercest storms, only to find myself awake in my reading chair at home, with some gentle volume open on my lap. On cliffs, I galloped, waiting for the fit that would send *him* tumbling to the earth. I tried to maim him. I held needles to my eye, hoping that with my seizure, he would twitch. I noosed my rope—he retained me. I lit a match—he blew it out. With my razor, I touched the twinned pulse of our carotids, the beat of our eight-chambered heart. His hand clasped mine. My tears fell from his eyes.

I had no February, Sirs.

And now I am grown tired. (A week separates these lines.)

Servus thrives. With each convulsion I wake to find myself a less familiar man. Dead, stuffed grouse and staghorns decorate the place that I once called my home. Coming to, I feel hunting songs fading from my lips, their tunes briefly crossing our threshold before dying out. Sometimes, awaking with the brush of Constance's breath against my cheek, I believe, briefly, that I have returned to stay, only to be swept away again for weeks. Strangely, I am no longer afraid. Have I reconciled myself to my fate? Or is this simply the course of my affliction? Having claimed my wife, my February, my April, has he now come to take my fears? Or is it simply that my lucid intervals, like the briefest of encores, are too ephemeral for terror to take hold? I know not. Perhaps you, Gentlemen, can tell me. For now, I hasten to the post, lest Cain appear and confiscate this cry. I pray that if I am to lose my June, my August—if the year turns before I awake—I still might one day find your answer in the dusty journals of the County Association Library. Or will you too abandon me? Will you dismiss me as but a seizure in *his* mind? Will you rejoice, Sirs, as he advances, steadily, toward cure?

THE MIRACULOUS DISCOVERY
OF PSAMMETICHUS I

1.

Now, the Egyptians, before the reign of Psammetichus, believed themselves to be the most ancient race of mankind. But Psammetichus, upon ascending to the throne, set out to determine who truly was the most primitive. Finding it impossible to do so by dint of inquiry, he contrived the following method of discovery. Taking two children of the common sort, he gave them to a herdsman to raise, charging him to let no one utter a word in their presence, but to keep them in a secluded cottage, introducing only milk goats so that they might slake their thirst. His intention was to know, after the babblings of infancy were over, what word they would first articulate. And so it happened.

The herdsman obeyed his orders for two years, until one day, when he opened the door to the cottage, the children ran to him with outstretched arms and shouted, "Becos." At first the herdsman took no notice, but soon the word was constantly in their mouths. So he informed his lord, and Psammetichus commanded them to be brought into his presence. And having himself heard them pronounce "becos," he made inquiries into which people might use this word, and learned that "becos" was the Phrygian name for bread. Thus the Egyptians yielded their claims and admitted the greater antiquity of the Phrygians.

These were the real facts I learned at Memphis from the priests of Hephaistos. The Greeks, among other foolish tales, relate a different version, namely that Psammetichus sent the boys to live with women whose tongues he had removed.

—Herodotus, *The Histories,* Book II
(adapted from the translation by G. Rawlinson, 1858)

2.

Now it is said that Psammetichus, upon discovering the origin of human speech, did not rest but pushed forth in other inquiries. After unifying Egypt and liberating her from the yoke of Assyrian rule, he came to be blessed with hours of leisure in which to contemplate the mysteries of the world. And so it was that, sitting in his gardens, he found himself bewitched by the chattering of parrots. Now, having discovered the antiquity of Phrygian, he began to wonder if in fact the birds might speak an even older tongue. Thus he betook the following method of experiment. He selected a pair of newborn children from two fisherwomen and gave them to his aviarist to raise amongst his flocks with the following instructions: no one was to utter a word in their presence, they should be given birdseed for their hunger and perches for their sleep, and so be raised to think that they were fowl. And everything turned out as planned, for the aviarist followed his orders for three and a half years, upon which Psammetichus had the children captured in a net and taken to the palace, where they were educated in Egyptian. And they were brought before him, and he inquired, "What now do the birds speak of?" The boys crouched and blinked, and one licked a flea from his armpit, and the other scraped his teeth back and forth against the floor. Whereupon Psammetichus asked again, and the boys replied that the song sparrows spoke nostalgically of the berries in Ethiopia, and the peacocks of their own beauty, and the parrots of what the aviarist did with Psammetichus's favorite queen. From this Psammetichus learned of memory and vanity and to trust neither Lydian wives, nor aviarists from Krokodilopolis.

This is generally held to be a lesser discovery than the first, but one with more practical application.

3.

And Psammetichus, say the priests, did not relent in his search for knowledge. Pondering the truths unveiled by his questions, he came to understand the mistake of having studied such an idle prattler. And so he again made a tour of his menagerie, peering into the cages, stopping at last before a troop of gorillas, captured during the southern expeditions of his father, Necho I. Now this animal, which I have seen myself, is very much like a man, save that the organs of generation are placed in the back like those of a horse, though the teats are in the front. And Psammetichus must have also had this observation in mind, for he stopped before a she-gorilla, who had just brought to term a child, and was tending it with all the affection of a human mother, nursing and growling to it in a distinct yet incomprehensible tongue. And Psammetichus carefully prepared a new experiment. On the outskirts of Saïs, he had ramparts constructed around a jungle and inside them he let loose the troop. Then he selected two newborn children from the hairiest of Scythians, set them down inside the ramparts, and quickly closed the gates. And after not many hours, the she-gorilla arrived, sniffed at the infants, and, grabbing one by the leg, dashed it against the ground as if it were a doll. But finding the other to her liking, she treated it with the same tenderness she had shown her own, placing it at her breast and disappearing into the forest. And everything turned out as planned, for after five years, Psammetichus sent his hunters into the gardens, where they ambushed the troop, killing them all. But the child they did not harm: he was captured and brought back to Saïs, where he was bathed and cured of grunting and public defecation and at last educated in the Egyptian tongue. Then the boy was conveyed to Psammetichus's chamber, and the king asked him, "What stories have you learned from those apes?" And the boy, glowering from beneath a heavy brow, made answer: "Come, I will tell you." Whereupon the king knelt to receive the secret, and with one swift lunge the boy bit off his ear and leapt onto the throne, proceeding to chew the flesh slowly, with hatred in his eyes. From this experiment, Psammetichus learned little about the language of animals, but much about experimental design.

4.

Now Egypt had long been closed to foreigners, and alien vessels were banned from entering any of the Nile's mouths. But Psammetichus, having employed thousands of Greek mercenaries to drive off the Assyrians, granted these men free movement to and from their homeland. And so it was that the trade between Greeks and Egyptians grew, and Greek temples were erected, and Egypt sent alum and corn to Greece, and Greece sent philosophers to Egypt. Now these men, rather than teaching the king Truth, as he'd desired, could not agree on anything. So Psammetichus had a new wing of the palace built next to his own so that they might resolve their differences. And day in and day out the philosophers spoke of whether men were good or evil, but they *did* nothing. At last Psammetichus, tired of such womanly lassitude, devised an experiment to answer their question once and for all. This time, he selected three newborn children of boatmen and gave them to a swine-herd with the following instructions. One child was to be raised as normal and taught to do good, while the second was to be taught the reverse: namely, that one should murder and steal and lie and engage in all other sorts of filth that is shocking to the gods. The third child would be raised wild among the pigs. And I was told that when the children were three years old they were all brought to the palace, where one by one they were placed in a room with a kitten, a coin, and a piece of bread. As had been fore-seen, the child raised in goodness stroked the little kitten, fed it the bread (even softening it with the moisture of his own mouth), and made gentle inquiries as to whom the coin belonged. Next, the child raised against the law was brought into the room. Immediately, he killed the kitten, pocketed the coin, and ate the bread. When he was asked as to the fate of the coin and bread, he said they were eaten by the kitten. Finally the last child, the wild one raised by pigs, was summoned. He ate the bread, tried to eat the coin, and played with the kitten. From this Psammetichus learned that the answer to whether man is good or evil is: inconclusive.

5.

And so it came that a queen of Psammetichus (a replacement) asked him, "Whence this inquisitiveness?" After all, the court was full of priests and philosophers. Couldn't they provide him with his answers? And stroking this creature's plump and comely cheek, Psammetichus fed her a date on his smallest finger, as was the girl's preference. And he told her the following story.

Not long after he had secured the throne, he had been vexed by a question of great material consequence, namely thus: what was the depth of the Nile? Taking a boat to the center of the river, he slowly lowered a rope on which knots were tied at regular intervals. Lower and lower it went, but it did not stop. He returned with a longer rope and repeated the experiment, but still it did not stop, though it was a thousand fathoms long. "The river was bottomless!" cried his queen, her mouth full of dates. But Psammetichus shook his head. That was what his counselors had claimed, but he, Psammetichus, had reasoned that the river current carried the rope downstream, so he was not measuring the river's depth but its length, an interesting question, certainly, but not the one he had set out to solve. That, he said, was why he no longer trusted his counselors, who had the intelligence of a fifteen-year-old bride, with none of the advantages.

And Psammetichus's queen beamed with admiration for the wisdom of her husband. But with the memory of this question left unanswered, a cloud had come across his face.

6.

And so Psammetichus completed his fiftieth year, and the entire kingdom celebrated, and there arrived gifts of mongooses and fireflies and more philosophers. But nothing could bring him pleasure, nor did all the clysters calm his mind. Then gateways were constructed in his honor, and everywhere there were processions and songs about kings of generations past. Yet who among his ancestors could give him pride? Cheops, who sacrificed the honor of his own daughter just to build his pyramids? Or Mykerinos, around whom swirled even nastier tales? Or Pheros, who threw a spear in anger at the Nile? The Nile! Indeed, it is said that Psammetichus was particularly irked by the story of Pheros, for he could not abide stupidity, and even the swineherds knew you didn't throw a spear at the Nile, lest the gods curse you with a blindness that must be treated with the water of a woman who had lain only with her husband—a cure that rarely worked, as such women were so hard to find.

Similarly, they say, he took little joy in his heir, Necho II. But it was not always so, for Psammetichus, over many years, had prayed to have a son. Night and day, he practiced intercourse, but his ministrations yielded up no child, for all his wives were barren, all twenty-eight. Now on the outskirts of Saïs, there is a place that I have seen myself, where cows are buried with their horns protruding above the ground. One day, Psammetichus, long before his experiments, was walking there when he began to weep, and his tears fell upon the earth. Because these cows are sacred to Isis, it came to pass that the goddess arrived to Psammetichus in a dream and promised him a son, a great man, a builder of canals. And such was his joy that despite having prayed daily for a companion who might share in the practice of memory or poesy, Psammetichus accepted one interested in irrigation. And to the wife named by Isis he explained further his joy thus: that even if the child was not bewitched by questions of history, perhaps together they might pursue mysteries of the natural world, such as why cats leap into fire, and how a phoenix could mold a giant egg of myrrh, if it hasn't any hands. Or at the very least, they might go walking by the Nile, as Psammetichus had done with *his* father, and turn over stones to see what creatures they could find.

And the boy was born, and time proved the Oracle right, for he was good at canals, though in truth, he was good at digging, not at planning. He dug canals in the streets and marketplace and in the gardens and the road to Elephantine. And even though he discovered how to cut through stone, he didn't understand the general principle that water flows from high to low, and so flooded the quarters of the concubines with the water from the Royal Pond. And Psammetichus, wakened from an afternoon slumber by a commotion, stood in silence behind the gesticulating crowd of philosophers, and watched with a heavy heart as his son shouted at the water and beat it with his staff and commanded his slave to do the same, while his cats clung terrified to the walls and ceiling, and his concubines screamed and fell about, their gowns soaked with pond scum and their collars with the kohl that had been painted hieroglyphically over their eyes. And observing the boy, Psammetichus thought, How could my miraculous seed have created this, I who saved Egypt, I who uncovered the oldest language in the world? And he took little consolation from the answer, which appeared to him thus: the aviarist from Krokodilopolis.

7.

And Psammetichus, it is said, came to wake in the night, shouting, "The end is coming soon!" Now the Egyptians believed that all human beings had a life force that would not perish with the death of the body, just as they believed that the king would one day join the gods. But Psammetichus found no consolation in such convictions. And I am told that the priests of Psammetichus tried to comfort him. At all hours they brought him ancient writings from the temples, and so, by reason, sought to prove the immortality of Psammetichus, repeating thus: that his mummified corpse would last until the end of time, and every year his family would bring food offerings to his tomb, and that there is no true death, for man lives forever in the glory of his children. And just as the priests had proclaimed this, I am told Necho II entered the chamber, naked save a wreath of flowers tied about his privy member, carrying a shovel in his right hand and an ibis in his left. Whereupon followed a long silence. Then the king made to depart, and the head priest, who had learned the art of rhetoric from the philosophers, called him back, reminding the other priests that it was not the *family* who truly tended to the tomb of the king, but rather the *caste of priests* themselves, the most learned men in all of Egypt. And another priest said, "Do not fear death, for your brains will be pulled out through your nostrils and your belly slit and washed with palm wine and filled with cassia and frankincense." And another counseled thus: that among the gods Psammetichus would learn all the answers that he sought. But, as I have shown, Psammetichus could find no comfort in that which could not be proved by rigorous experimentation. As for the promise of eternal worship, he asked his priests, "Does anyone worship Neferkare III?" Then they looked dumbly at each other and tried to speak of other matters, for none recalled the name of this king who ruled for only four years, seventeen dynasties ago. And Psammetichus, who wished to have no more to do with them, said, "Look it up."

8.

Now, concerning the final years of Psammetichus, I have heard from my informants in Memphis that his longings for knowledge grew so sharp that he fell into a frenzy, and some even claimed he was possessed. But since I do not respect men's conclusions with regard to human sentiments, I sought a female opinion from the prophetess of Dodona. And she told me that it was not possession, but rather a fluttering moth that a sorcerer had placed inside his chest. But I did not believe this either, for the inside of the body is moist, and no one has ever observed a moth in water; more likely it was a fish.

Now, despite such disagreements, everyone I have spoken to is of accord with regard to the history that followed: that Psammetichus sent out his messengers to collect newborn children from all corners of his kingdom, placing them amongst the islands in that part of the Nile known as the

Canopic mouth. And there he built many enclosures, the ruins of which can still be seen today. Then men who once had been bricklayers or scorpion charmers or who had specialized in capturing animals for mummification gave up their work to devote themselves to the experiments of Psammetichus. And some children he raised among geese and some among wild dogs; and some he raised in solitude or in packs, and some hanging upside down so that he might know if they could distinguish between down and up. This I have heard from Thebes, while in Memphis they tell me other tales: that Psammetichus commanded some children to be raised thinking water was wine and wine water, and some boys he raised amidst old hags who were called "beautiful," while nubile young maidens were shunned. And others he taught that dreams were real and it was the waking life that was illusory.

This I heard in Memphis and Thebes. In Dodona, the prophetesses say that it was Psammetichus who answered the mystery of why some people weave by pushing the woof up and others by pulling it down, and what is fear, and why some people love to believe nonsense, for example that ibises kill flying serpents, when no one had ever seen a flying serpent, not once.

★　★　★

9.

Now as the children came of age, Psammetichus gathered them in his palace. There were hundreds then, some say even thousands. But regardless of what he learned, he wasn't satisfied, as if there remained, beneath it all, a single question beyond his reach. And there are many opinions on what he was seeking, most of which I don't have space to relate here, but some state that Psammetichus wouldn't stop until he understood the antiquity of man, and others that it was the source of all stories that intrigued him, and others the thoughts of infants in the womb. But I, who have observed that men with many questions are driven by an emptiness inside them, know that he was searching even deeper. And this was the opinion that I expressed to the prophetess of Dodona. Whereupon she asked me what I thought was the question that so tormented him, and I made answer that it was this: What is Psammetichus? Or to put it otherwise: Who of these quiet, quaking children is Psammetichus? What was I before they bound me to this throne, these gods, this tongue?

And I knew I was correct, for the prophetess didn't dispute me, but said, "What is Herodotus?" and a small fish leapt inside my chest.

★ ★ ★

10.

Now regarding the end of the reign of Psammetichus, there are many lies told, some saying that he took poison, and others that he had his son murdered and he himself lived for another forty years under the name Necho II. I do not believe any of these tales, but rather that which was told to me in Memphis and confirmed by those I interviewed in Heliopolis, namely that, with his mind full of answers and his palace with children, Psammetichus couldn't sleep. And every night he was seen to go to the darkness of his gardens, where the children gathered, and there he watched them as they chattered like geese, or hung upside down from the branches, or lowered their faces to drink water from his fountains, or wrestled and played, or tasted the earth, or just sat and held themselves about the shoulders, swaying back and forth for hours, staring sadly at the moon. And when he ventured forth among them, there were those who shrank away, and others who came and clasped his legs, and still others who leapt into his arms, took his hand, and pressed it to their eyes and mouths as if they wished to tell him something, but they had never learned to speak.

Now Psammetichus knew that the priests were already preparing for his passage into the afterlife, for the carts of animals were arriving, and the embalming ointments gave off sweet smells that wafted through the palace, and the corridors echoed with the cries of the fortunate slaves honored to serve him on his journey down. But when his counselors came and asked him which of his wives he wished to accompany him, he didn't answer. Instead, he commanded that his throne be carried to the Nile, so that he might watch the river. And those who have related this story to me say that all the citizens of Saïs gathered to see him, but that he paid them no heed, and stayed there five days and nights until he expired. There are other versions, told to me by tricky and poetic men, that he was last heard singing to himself in a barbarian tongue, while others claim that it was not the body of Psammetichus in the tomb I observed at Saïs, but rather an empty mummy, and that the king did not expire in his chair, but rather rose and, gathering stones in his hands, descended slowly, without fear, into the river's still unfathomed depths.

ON GROWING FERNS AND OTHER PLANTS IN GLASS CASES, IN THE MIDST OF THE SMOKE OF LONDON

1.

Sometimes, during the night, she wakes to a presence, a creature sliding through the darkness, watching, waiting to descend. She doesn't dare to look; to move even slightly is to risk waking the child, and it's for him she knows the ghost has come. There is nothing she can do but remain in utter stillness, beside the boy, so close that she can feel his exhalations on her cheek.

Watching, as his blankets softly rise and fall, and the shadows stir around them, and the dim light plays against the pale blue paper on the wall.

She can hear it then, the boy's breath quickening as the ghost draws closer. Very faintly, from deep within his chest, the tickling of a wheeze. Just a whisper, but she has become a great student of his breathing, an expert. She knows, then, what is coming. The boy so peaceful now, and yet in seconds, the ghost will be upon him, he will lurch awake, tearing at his sheets, his chest heaving as he throws his covers from the bed. Desperately, she will try to calm him, but to no avail. She will pray: that this attack won't be the final one, that it will pass as all the others, that the earth will continue on its turning, bringing spring and warmth, the end of winter burning, and perhaps, if fortune smiles, their escape.

A patterning of raindrops at the window...a shift in the room's currents...and the wraith halts in its descent. Now, from above, she senses a retreat, the dark smoke whisking back in viscous eddies. Inches away, William's breath slows again and softens. The wheezing vanishes. For a moment—another hour, perhaps the night—the danger has passed.

The attacks—paroxysms, the doctors would call them, though there was no mistaking the focused violence of the assaults—had begun the previous winter, when the boy was six. For half as many years, since her husband's accident and death, they had been living with her sister Katherine in Finsbury, in the spare room on the third floor. Elizabeth had not intended to remain with them so long. Her sister had a family, a husband with a growing reputation, and—now that their two sons were away at school—a social life requiring careful cultivation. And yet where was she to go? Beyond some distant relations in Herefordshire, Katherine *was* her family. And even if Katherine were concerned solely with others' opinions, it would have been quite indelicate for her to cast her sister out.

Of course, no one had spoken of reputation; these were Elizabeth's worries, and ones that plagued her mostly in the moments of her doubt. In fact, Katherine had welcomed her with warmth, and Charles, who himself had grown up without a father, treated William with—if not the attention he had given his own children—affection nonetheless. This wasn't difficult. William was an easy child: thoughtful, quiet, compliant in his studies, with a beguiling deference, as if he had never outgrown the sense of having just arrived in that new, unfamiliar house. As each morning Charles departed early for the firm, the sisters took breakfast together, while the boy ate at a second, smaller table a few feet away. This was followed by an hour of bathing and dressing, and another reviewing his lessons before the arrival of his tutor. In the afternoon, after the man's departure, William would clamber into his mother's lap and recount that day's Latin or mathematics. She had little interest in either, but it didn't matter, for she was happy just to look at him, so much like her husband, with Edward's mop of flax-brown hair, and Edward's arching, impish eyebrows, and a long, sloping neck that gave his high, stiff collar a dandyish air.

And they would read together, or play a game of chess or draughts, or head out into the city to explore. Which was where, that December morning, three days before the turn of the year, the problems began.

Later, questioned by the doctors, she would wonder if the illness hadn't started earlier. Certainly, she had heard him wheezing, coughing. Certainly, there were times when, hurtling up the staircase, he'd grown short of breath. But this was London, after all, and at the peak of Industry. Everywhere were forges and manufactories, tanyards, dyers, iron foundries, glassworks, breweries with their plumes of dark, thick smoke. Once, looking over her shoulder at an illustration of Mount Etna, William, age four then, had pointed at the volcanic vents and shouted, "The Docklands!" Who *didn't* cough and wheeze? Alone, discreetly spitting into her handkerchief, she found it specked with grit, and there were days, if the potash kilns were burning, that tears ran down her cheeks. Morwenna, the housemaid, often disappeared to distant rooms to hide her fits of hacking. At the butcher's, in the piles of pink sheep pluck, the lungs of city animals were black and half the price.

Had she noticed? the doctors asked. Yes, but in the way she noticed everything about her son. The way he twisted his fingers around one another when he was thinking. The way, when he thought she wasn't looking, he skipped the page in *Robinson Crusoe* with the engraving of the savages. The way that, still, in haste, he sometimes put the left shoe on the right. So: yes, a cough, at times, at times a shortness of breath. But this was true for all of them; no, she never believed him to be sick.

December, then, the city sodden with Christmas toddy, hearth fires lolling the ash of sea coal into the Thames fog, the sugar mills reburning. That day they had been up near Clerkenwell, on an errand, when, passing through the dark exhalations of a forge, William, bundled deep in coat and scarf, began to wheeze. It was an inhuman sound; for an instant, she mistook it for the hissing of a steam valve. But then she turned to see him doubled over, hands on his knees, chest heaving.

She fell to him, skirts pooling across the cobbles.

Another whinny, this equine, and bearing down beneath a whip. She swept her son up and carried him out of the black cloud and through the nearest door, into a tavern, where for the next half hour, beneath a lurid painting of gambling monkeys in cuffs and pirate hats, William slowly, very slowly, regained his breath.

And then he was well, laughing at the monkeys, one of whom, she realized with a start, was rustling a free hand up the frilled skirts of a monkey wench. Time to go! But at the door she paused, gauging the sifting soot that drifted past the window. And if it happened again?

she wondered. She didn't note it then, but that moment marked a beginning. Of a new vigilance, a division of the world, into places where William could breathe and those he couldn't.

But how else were they to get back home? She took her shawl and wrapped his head so that only his eyes were visible. He watched her, puzzled. "Because of the smoke," she whispered, as if *it* could hear her, too.

The second attack came two weeks later, on Ludgate Hill, in the grey pall sliding from the ranks of terrace chimneys. The third, the following morning, when he leapt over a shattered hogshead in the street outside their house. Both short, mercifully so, the shock of the first onslaught now replaced by a gnawing recognition of a new, tenacious presence in their lives. Still, she said nothing about it to Katherine or Charles. She would not worry them, she told herself. It was a passing cold, an inflammation, perhaps a mild "asthma" he would outgrow. For as long as she recalled, her father, stout and hearty, had regularly suffered a late summer tightness that he spoke of almost amiably as his "little 'heeze."

There was another shadow to this thought, she knew, which was that she *couldn't* trouble Katherine or Charles. That when they had taken her in, it was with the understanding that she would bring no complications. That her mourning would never pass into hysterics. That the boy, pattering gaily down the stairs, reciting Virgil, would remain a gift, and not a burden, someone who brought joy into their home.

And then the fourth attack, in Bloomsbury, where, on the occasion of William's seventh birthday, the four of them had made a celebratory excursion to the Museum.

They were in the Egyptian hall when it happened. All morning, getting ready, she had sensed a slight whistle to his breath, but the air was particularly foul that day, an oily coal smoke, dull as aspic, which sifted through the antique glazing of the windows and left a scrim upon the sills. Her own eyes burned as they walked through an amber haze, even Katherine was coughing, and by the time they reached the Museum, all of them were complaining of a soreness in their throats. But the galleries had brought relief, and they were progressing toward the mummies when William, unable to restrain himself, bolted forward eagerly, only to draw up short as if someone had punched him in the chest. Instantly, Elizabeth was at his side, but when she touched him, he pushed her hand away. Palms braced against his knees. Shoulders rigid, eyes wide, nostrils flaring. Even in the dim hall, the cold air, she could see drops of perspiration beading on his forehead, a gathering pallor to his skin.

By then Katherine and Charles had reached them. *William? Elizabeth, what's happening?* But the answer was there before them, sucking at the air, chin jutting like the horrid rictus of a gargoyle, the muscles in his neck pulled taut.

The attack lasted nearly two hours. They moved him from the center of the room and to a bench. A crowd gathered; a doctor was summoned—or promised, for none came. From time to time, a helpful citizen urged the curious to "give the boy some space." But to Elizabeth, all this was happening as if at a distance. It seemed as though William was so intent on breathing that he was unaware of anything around him, and she was unaware of anything but him. His belly bellowed with each heaving, and when at last the ghost released him from its coils, he gave a cry and crumpled into her lap.

It was dusk when they found themselves outside. There, the smell of heating coal sent her heart into another flurry, yet, thankfully, her son, asleep against her shoulder, didn't stir.

In a carriage on the way home, the three adults were silent. "We must send for a doctor," Katherine said at last, but Elizabeth protested. They didn't need a doctor. It was just the air, she said.

"It's not the air," said Katherine. "I breathe the air. There's something wrong with *him*."

Memories now of Edward broken by the calomel purges, retching, pleading for his doctor to stop.

But Charles agreed with Katherine. And he had

acquaintances in the Scientific Club: learned, experienced men who would know how to help.

2.

There would be three of them, three learned, experienced men: Watts of Hyde Park, and Moss of Harley Street, and Underwood of the Magdalen Hospital, an expert in diseases of women and childbirth, author of a popular book on physical culture and the raising of boys. One after the other, they climbed the stairs to the nursery, drew out their long stethoscopes from their traveling bags, listened, tapped, prodded, prescribed. The attacks, the fits of wheezing, were indeed symptoms of an asthma, they all concluded, addressing Charles, though they disagreed as to whether it was acute catarrhal asthma or dry catarrhal asthma, or mucous catarrhal asthma, or humoral asthma or pure nervous asthma or symptomatic nervous asthma, or just suffocative catarrh. And then the other possibilities they murmured in lower voices, these words long and Latinate, more like the scientific names for sea creatures than any disease Elizabeth knew. But nothing to worry about, not yet.

Three doctors! The thought of one had frightened her enough; had she known there would be three, she never would have consented. But their prescriptions, however different, all had the same effect: they only worsened William's breathing. The niter prescribed by Watts sent her son into fierce fits of coughing, as did the tobacco, the lobelia, the squills. Moss, in turn, dictated increasing doses of laudanum; when she told him, quietly, eyes lowered, that it had reduced her child to a state of confused, hallucinating languor, he thundered that she would rather have him dead. Underwood had nodded sagely when she told him of the others' failings. Of course: cure must be heroic; they hadn't done enough! The spasmodic constriction was dependent on an existing irritation of the mucous membrane of the air passages—this must be reckoned with, and forcefully. But she refused his recommendation of a bleeding. And it was only after another attack in late January that she consented to a "mild blistering," restraining William with a sickening sense of complicity as the doctor ground an azure fly into a gleaming powder and applied it to excoriations on the boy's bare chest. This did nothing but throw her son into a frenzy. Eyes wide and accusatory, screaming, *Mama, stop him,* unsure whether he should fight her or seek the shelter of her embrace.

There would be no more doctors, she told herself after this. The first two were proof enough of Medicine's uselessness; to believe that a third, a fourth, could cure him was lunacy. But Charles—good, kind Charles—persisted. For God, in constructing the world, had not done so with whimsy. In his twelve years as an engineer, Charles had seen nothing less than the forces of nature reduced down to their most basic forms. Monthly, at the meetings of the Club, he listened as mysteries were unraveled: light dissected into her spectra, electricity spawned by the movements of magnets. In comparison, asthma was nothing. Gravity had been conquered; balloons streamed skyward from the fields of Vauxhall. Lyell had explained the shifting of the continents. Herschel had made a map of Mars.

She couldn't disagree, of course. Charles was the man who let her son stand on a chair and peer into his micro-scope, who only chuckled when William was discovered to have added his own illustrations to a volume of *Britannica,* right on the very plates. She couldn't disagree: she'd seen what happened when Katherine attempted. How kindly and patient he could be! But it was like arguing with Reason itself.

Yet it was more than just Charles's authority that secured her acquiescence. William's illness, she understood, had begun to alter the unspoken terms of charity. Her gift to them had revealed itself as something broken. Or worse: a threat. For already, he was transforming their home from a place of hope and optimism into one of constant fear and worry. Into a hospital. Already she sensed a reluctance in her sister to host acquaintances. And how could she, when upstairs there was a child of such fragility that any dinner might be interrupted by a death?

And so it was that when Charles announced the visit

of a fourth doctor, an expert in the lungs and auscultation with whom he'd entered into correspondence, Elizabeth said nothing, just reasserted her resolve—there would be no bleeding, no fly, no squills. She would listen, but she wouldn't let anyone hurt her son.

The new doctor's name was Forbes. From her window, Elizabeth watched, fist tightening around the curtains, as the carriage pulled up outside their gate that day in early February, and three men in black descended from the cab.

They met in the parlour, a room of fading green wall-paper and green silk-upholstered furniture, where a dim light filtered through the sooted glass. The doctor was removing his gloves as she entered. He was flanked by his two apprentices, young men trussed soberly in sable stock ties, still silvered by the mist. Despite her instinctive an-tipathy to any man of Medicine, to her surprise she sensed her vigilance yield instantly with this new one. He was tall and older, with Grecian, windswept hair and a calm and quiet to his movements, and she was struck to find herself registering how handsome he was, with concerned blue eyes that studied her as if she were a person of importance. Then Charles directed her to her seat, and Katherine took William to an alcove on the far side of the room.

In contrast to Watts and Moss and Underwood, Forbes had many questions—endless questions, really. He wanted to know about the circumstances of each attack, the presence of similar afflictions in her family and that of her deceased husband, of all remedies attempted and their effects. At first, she was succinct in her answers. She worried that she was boring him. For all her love for William, she could not help wondering why this man, this expert, would devote himself so entirely to her son. There was the fee, of course, and the advantages to be gained from curing the nephew of a man like Charles Nash, just as there was—she apprehended as the exam progressed—a particular antipathy to Dr. Underwood. But it was more than this, for as the visit continued, she realized that Forbes already knew much of the story from Charles, and that he had been enticed there less by fee or fame than by the challenge of a particularly severe case. As if her boy were a specimen, offered up by Charles as currency in the great scientific exchanges. Like a rare fossil or the newest galvanic device.

For a moment, this thought broke her reverie, and Elizabeth looked away. Across the room, out of earshot, William was peering at a heavy volume, his hair falling into his eyes, his tie and jacket painting the very image of the scholar at work. How could anyone suggest he was anything but healthy? But now a new appreciation of the gravity of his condition was dawning. There was no doctor after Forbes, she knew. He was—to use the phrase—the *very end*. The end, and yet this word now appeared to her not with its usual sense of hopelessness, but rather: destination, even destiny. This man would care for him, for her, for them.

As if with his attentive questions, he was gathering up her fears and sadness and making them his own.

At last, it was time for the examination, and William was called over, asked to undress before a lantern. He was shaking; he, too, recalled the blistering. She drew him to her, stroking his hair, whispering promises that no one would hurt him, never again. She expected the doctor to scold her, but Forbes only smiled gently, without showing his teeth. When they were ready, he began with William's eyes and nose and mouth, his skin and hair, his nails, pausing only to note faint areas of rash. When at last one of the apprentices removed the stethoscope from its bag, he passed it to his master with the air of handing a scepter to a king. Forbes took it without ceremony, without a glance. It was a wooden tube, burnished with the craftsmanship of an oboe, half the length of those of Watts and Moss and Underwood, which now seemed to have been designed to keep their patients at a distance. As Forbes listened, his head was so close to William that wisps of the doctor's white hair brushed against the boy's chest. It tickled. For the first time, William smiled, then let out a nervous giggle, which Forbes silenced with a touch.

The room was still. The doctor's eyes were closed in concentration as he asked the boy to inhale and exhale, to take quick breaths and long ones, to cough, to lean forward, lift his arms...Watching, Elizabeth at first could only marvel at the beauty of the child, and her heart swelled with such pride that she reflexively touched her fingers to her throat. Something so perfect couldn't be flawed or broken. The proof was there in his slight, gently rising shoulders, in the way he looked around at everybody watching him, no longer trembling, now proud to be the object of such interest, a look of amusement on his lips. It was only as the exam proceeded that she let her eyes drift to the doctor. Inch by inch, she knew, her son's lungs were taking form again, in Forbes's imagination. What could he see? she wondered. She pictured clouds of exquisite carmine filigree, slowly lifting and falling. Until suddenly, across this scene, there flashed an image of sheep pluck, coal dark upon the butcher's floor.

At last, the doctor stopped.

"You may get dressed," he said. The boy abided, bound into his mother's lap.

Instead of addressing Charles, Forbes spoke to her.

"You have been given, I think, a diagnosis."

She nodded.

"My assessment is the same. I might add only that while Dr. Underwood, I believe, felt this to be catarrhal asthma, I would emphasize the component of a spinal irritation. But this is a matter only of degree. You have tried, Mr. Nash tells me, everything, save bleeding."

He must have anticipated her protest, because he raised a finger. "Such a course is not unexpected. There are few diseases less amenable to interference. But there is no need to expose the boy further to such torments. You may stop."

She held William closer, needing him near. Should she send him from the room? she wondered. Or would this only frighten him more? Forbes went on. "Perhaps if he continues to decline, we can discuss a treatment. For now, I have great confidence that with the avoidance of inciting stimuli, the asthmatic child may achieve a long life, even in so severe a case. This means stimuli both chemical and nervous. The diet must be bland. He must not be frightened, must avoid pain or overexcitement. He must not laugh too much or breathe too deeply. Above all, he must keep from taking cold."

She nodded in understanding. This was good, wasn't it? she thought. He might achieve a long life! There was hope, then. Why did she feel as though she would cry?

Outside the high window, the far side of the street was obscured by haze. Cautiously, she asked, "And if the air itself is a stimulus?"

Forbes nodded, for this was what he was coming to. "Then he must avoid the air."

The solution, of course, was that they must leave London, and as soon as possible. Quickly, Katherine and Charles fell into making arrangements. Charles had an aunt in Newhaven, in Sussex, by the sea. A letter was sent, an answer received. By good fortune, there was a room to spare; his aunt could use an extra hand, though Elizabeth should understand that life would be simple, without the diversions of the city. As for the boy, there were many such refugees in Newhaven who had found the sea air salubrious. The aunt asked only that Elizabeth comport herself as a widow, and not a woman who was "unattached."

Listening to Katherine and Charles discuss her departure, Elizabeth sensed a rising enthusiasm; they wished to help, she thought, but they were also relieved to be free of William's sickness, to return to hosting dinners, unhaunted by the wheezing child in the pale blue room above. And she, too, was relieved, by the prospect of departure, of no longer being a burden to her sister, of building a new life, a simpler life, at last.

Preparations progressed quickly. They would travel by private carriage to the Whale Inn in Southwark, where they would get the morning mail coach to Brighton, and from there proceed to Newhaven by the coast road. Charles and Katherine would come along. It would do them good to pass a week in the country, they said, though Elizabeth could not help but feel that they were escorting her out. The day arrived, they woke early, bags were hurried to the carriage. William, who had been plied with promises of seashells and shipwrecks, had dressed himself with an extra ribbon around his waist: her natty little buccaneer. He nearly tumbled down the stairs in excitement. Elizabeth wanted to restrain him, to keep him from overexertion, as Forbes had warned. But it was hard not to feel that their flight was an adventure rather than a doctor's solemn order. As they entered the carriage, a wind was blowing from the north, clearing the skies ever so slightly, and the street glittered in the light of sunrise. How bright it all was! Columns of yellow tallow glowed in a chandler's window, green alfalfa dusted the plum tights of the driver, and when they stopped, little boys pushed fistfuls of carnations against the glass. A smile passed between Elizabeth and Katherine. Charles hummed. They were just crossing Blackfriars Bridge, with the factories of Southwark arrayed before them, when the boy began to wheeze.

3.

There have been complications, Charles wrote that evening to Dr. Forbes. *The child is too delicate, the coal smoke too pervasive. The trip had to be suspended.* Perhaps with summer and the end of winter burning, they could try again.

They were sitting in the parlour, at the same table at which the doctor had carried out his examination. Upstairs, William was sleeping, exhausted; the attack had lasted much of the morning, and they had been forced into another public house to get shelter from the soot. Dazed, Elizabeth watched as Charles folded the letter. How simple it all seemed as he described it! The child was too delicate. And yes, of course, they'd try again.

But the trip had marked a change. Not only by the violence with which the attack descended upon him in the carriage. Not only by the horror of his fishlike thrashing against the walls, the sounds of her sister screaming. Not only by the choking supplications, or the cold in William's fingers as she grasped his hand.

Instead, the full realization would come later that night, when, at last returning to the room, pausing above the sleeping child, Elizabeth had leaned across the bed to kiss his forehead, and felt the faint thrum of his wheezing on her lips, and understood the ghost, the great constrictor, had followed them home.

Doctor Forbes's reply was swift, affirmative, and girded with recipes, for inhaled stramonium and a tincture of poppies, to calm the boy and help him rest.

"Summer, then!" said Charles, radiating determination. And they would travel north, and make a great loop and so avoid the mills of Southwark altogether. Perhaps the warmer weather would come early that year. They might even try in May, just three months off.

And Reason had spoken, flexed its muscles. It was simple, a matter of seasons, winds. Why then did she accept Morwenna's saucers of vinegar, the dried ear of a donkey sent for from Cornwall, the spar stones the maid enclosed in a little bag around William's wrist? For could he make it to May? Every morning, Elizabeth awoke to find someone thinner, paler. He hardly ate. In her dreams at night—the same dreams that conjured up enchanted corridors coursing through the sulfurous fog—he slurped ravenously at glistening stews. But the doctor had warned against anything rich or salted, and William pushed away the tepid clabber Morwenna delivered to their room. He moved as if his whole body were very heavy. By the time February finally turned to March, sapped by the fits at night, by the poppy tincture, he scarcely left his bed.

She read to him. One by one, she brought out all his favorites: a children's Ovid, *Crusoe,* books of science, and illustrated fairy tales. But how different these stories seemed now! Watching him out of the corner of her eye, she found herself wondering what he thought of them: the mocking vision of a crystal carriage, these fables of children consumed by witches, of mothers offering their firstborn to malicious goblins?

These metamorphoses. A girl transformed into a laurel tree, a crocus, a galloping heifer.

A boy into a murmuring brook.

For I saw the sea come after me as high as a great hill, and as furious as an enemy, which I had no means or strength to contend with: my business was to hold my breath, and raise myself upon the water if I could; and so, by swimming, to preserve my breathing, and pilot myself towards the shore, if possible, my

greatest concern now being that the sea, as it would carry me a
great way towards the shore when it came on, might not carry
me back again . . .

Let us read something different, she said to him, but
by mid-month, he was sleeping much of the day. Alone
then, she tried to turn her mind from the thoughts that
rose up from the darkness. The blame was hers: she had
done something to deserve this. Other times, she felt the
needle shift and point toward him. If he didn't get so
frightened. If he ate the food Morwenna prepared for
him. There must be some solution, some secret he knew
the answer to, some reason they had been imprisoned in
their tower, in their room of pale blue paper, that parody
of the sky they couldn't see. Didn't he wonder? Didn't
he ask himself why his life had become so unlike that of
other children? Was that why he couldn't carry himself to
the window and look out? For she couldn't bear to see
them either, hated them, hated all the healthy. Hated the
city, dreamed that a great quake would come and flatten
the factories and mills.

Oh to be free of such terrible ruminations! But her sleep
was increasingly plagued by them, and she could hardly
focus long enough to read a book. All she could manage,
really, was to thumb, distractedly, through back issues of
Katherine's magazines: women's journals and literary quar-
terlies, but mostly a pair of gardening monthlies, which,
with their lists of cultivars, and illustrations of planters

overflowing with pelargoniums and moneywort, offered, if briefly, an escape:

"A Report upon the best Varieties of Gooseberry."

"A new Descriptive Catalogue of Roses."

"A Note upon the Black Corinth Grape."

And then one day in late March, midway through one of the issues: "On growing Ferns and other Plants in Glass Cases, in the midst of the Smoke of London; and on transplanting Plants from one Country to another, by similar Means."

William turned. Would she sing to him?

"In a moment, sweetheart. Hush."

It was but two pages, wedged between an article on Cape heaths and a "Descriptive Notice of the Gardens of Misses Garnier at Wickham," this filled with exquisite images of rose-lined pathways and trellised garden seats. The author was one "N. B. Ward, Esq." of Wellclose Square in White-chapel, and his article began with an account of how, for many years an avid gardener, he had long dreamed of noth-ing greater than to have, in the garden of his London home, an old wall covered with ferns and mosses. Many times he had tried to transplant species collected in the woods, but all had died, killed no doubt by smoke blasting from the nearby manufactories. He had all but given up hope when one day, in a glass bottle in which he was trying to hatch a chrysalis, he spied tiny specks of vegetation, which soon revealed themselves to be a species of *Poa* and a *Nephrodium* fern. For the subsequent three years, the plants flourished on his windowsill, dying only when the cap to the bottle rusted and rainwater flooded in. Following this, he had repeated the experiment with over sixty fern species—and here he listed the genera: *Adiantum, Aspidium, Asplenium, Blechnum, Cheilanthes, Davallia, Dicksonia, Doodia, Grammitis, Hymenophyllum, Lycopodium, Nephrodium, Niphobolus, Polypodium, Pteris, Trichomanes*—as well as flowering plants such as anemone and veronica, all with great success. Indeed, he had stayed up one night watching mushrooms growing in one of his vessels, and had kept, for weeks, in a large glass case closed with oiled silk a very happy songbird, a species no longer seen in the city, further proving that the effects of smoke were the same on the leaves of plants as on the lungs of animals, and that even the most delicate species could thrive if protected from the London air. It was simply necessary that the cases be sealed so as to allow for the diffusion of gas but not soot, after which there was no reason to suppose that their Edenic contents could not persist *ad infinitum*. And one could imagine the many applications, from the collection of fragile specimens in far-off Brazil or Van Diemen's Land, to the brightening effect that such boxes might have on the dreary lodgings of the poor, provided Parliament rescind the onerous tax on glass and…

There was more, but by now her fingers were shaking so hard she had to stop.

4.

Bye, baby Bunting,
Mother's gone a-hunting,
Gone to get a lion's skin
To wrap the baby Bunting in.

5.

Who of you recall that night in March in 1836? The cold, the mist, the Thames wind sweeping through the alleyways, carrying the knocking of the ships' hulls, the creaking of the wharfs? Who remembers the way the lanterns winked, the broth that slipped down from the smokestacks? Who heard, among the thousands of footsteps, the patter of a haunted figure, hood drawn closely about her neck? Who saw her hurrying, breaking into a run? Down Bishopsgate, down Houndsditch, down Aldgate, into Whitechapel's streets?

Did you wonder where she was racing, skin hot, eyes gleaming with tears brought on by weeping, by the sulfur suspended in the fog? Did you think her mad, to brave this night?

Who was there? In Finsbury, in Bishopsgate, in Whitechapel? For someone must have seen her, must have pointed her the way. Was it you who led her? Or did she find it on her own, that house behind the sailors' church, the windows green with life?

6.

And at the door, a brass knocker in the form of fiddleheads.

The clanking echoed up the stairs.

Silence. Then more knocks, urgent. Then: more lights, footsteps.

"Yes?"

It was a maid, a girl with bright red cheeks, a glow that seemed to emanate from the home itself.

"I wish to speak with Mr. Ward about his cases."

"Mr. Ward?"

Mr. N. B. Ward, Esq. She realized that she didn't even know his Christian name.

The girl pulled a shawl more closely about her shoulders. "It's nearly midnight. Is he expecting you?"

And, bewitched, Elizabeth answered, "Yes."

But such is the power of enchantment that the girl didn't question her, led her up a long stairway into a room of such green light as to leave her blinking. There were palms and figs, creepers spilling from their planters, climbing vines and profusions of mosses pressing wetly against their glass enclosures. And ferns, ferns everywhere, suspended from the ceiling, crowding the windowsills, cases upon cases. The maid departed, but Elizabeth didn't even notice. Now, flushed, still breathless from her haste, she drifted through the plants as if dreaming, the words of the monthly intoning like a hymn. *Adiantum, Aspidium, Asplenium*...The narrow path seemed to lead deeper within the grove, until at last she stopped before a great capsule, set on a table and towering nearly two feet above her head. Condensation on the inside of the glass caught the chandelier light, illuminating an explosion of ferns, dark green and emerald, with pale lime stalks curling from their hearts. And in the center of the tableau, and rising from a stone above the rest: a species she had never seen before, frilled, fimbriate, the end of its fronds fine to translucence, its lace hairs glistening with drops of water. Despite the glass that separated her from the plants, she could taste the moisture in the air.

From somewhere behind her, she heard two sets of footsteps, then the voice of the maid.

"Here, sir. She says you were expecting her."

The other didn't answer. In the reflection in the glass, Elizabeth watched a dark figure approaching through the leaves and vines. It was her moment to speak, she knew, her moment to explain her haste, her breathless midnight pilgrimage, her petition. But now that it was time, the words available to her were mocking. *This crystal carriage, this corridor, this lion's skin*. Ashamed by her impudence, her lie, her desperation, she couldn't speak. For what, in truth, was she to say? That Providence had led her to that issue of the *Gardener's Monthly*? That even Ward's own name seemed to be a sign sent to her, with its suggestion of both a hall for convalescence and a child in another's care? That together, that very night, they could begin to assemble the house of glass, the crystal carriage, that would transport her son to the sea air where he might breathe? Gently, Reason scolded her with its paternal chuckle, kind but firm. For who, what, had led her there, stumbling through the dark streets of Bishopsgate and Whitechapel? What madness, Elizabeth? Come home.

Deep within her pocket, her fingers released the torn pages of the *Monthly* and rose to touch the glass.

"Trichomanes speciosum," said Nathaniel Bagshaw Ward behind her. "From the woods of Killarney—it is the most delicate of the bristle ferns. Can you see how it is thriving?"

My mother turned. My mother could.

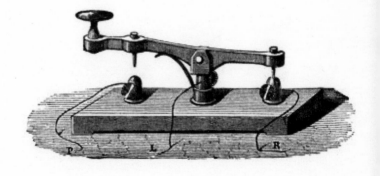

THE LINE AGENT PASCAL

Every morning, Hippolyte Pascal, agent of the Line at Urupá, woke to the sun and the sound of parrots, rose from his hammock, dressed, set a battered kettle on the fire, and crossed his tiny station to check the signal.

At 0600, if the Line was in order, he would receive the first transmission from the Depot, followed shortly by the second from the agent at Várzea Nova, eighty-two kilometers into the interior, and the third, from Juá. Then he would reply, PASCAL, URUPA, and the hour, and the others would answer in turn: Fernandes, fifty-eight kilometers forward at Itiraca, Bonplan at Macunarímbare, Wilson-Jones at Canaã, the Jesuit Perez at the Mines. The report would come next, minor variations on the previous morning: a band of Nambikwara sighted near Bonplan's station, a rotted telegraph pole at Itiraca, a call for fresh provisions, a request for gunpowder. And then he would rise and pour himself his coffee and set about his day.

Hippolyte Pascal had been a station agent for nine years. It was rare to find a man who could keep his post for so long. Some succumbed to disease, some to the violence of the jungle, some simply to the isolation, the horror of the vastness, the ceaseless shrill. Yet the territory, as it appeared to Pascal, bore small resemblance to the map. Because it was impossible to see beyond one or two paces into the forest that surrounded the station clearing, it mattered little whether civilization was one kilometer away or one thousand. What mattered was the Line. Sometimes he thought: it is as if they are next door, for when I speak, they listen, and they need only to call out and I'll respond. There were few men, he told himself, in such immediate contact with other people. Other days he thought, with an exhilaration that was almost dizzying: I am the loneliest man in the world.

The station house had been built by his predecessor, a German who had died of snakebite. Over time, Pascal had widened the windows to take in more of the forest and added a layer of palm fronds to the roof, which cooled the room and softened the monsoon rains that could turn the tin into a deafening drum. Inside there was a hammock strung between the walls, a chair, and a table upon which sat the apparatus of key and sounder, two crouching dragons of zinc and copper. The table's legs stood in tins of water, to keep away the ants. A single drawer held a razor and a pair of scissors and a vial of lavender oil he combed into his mustache. He kept both house and person as clean as the telegraph, wearing and washing his two white shirts on alternating days. In the pocket of his waistcoat was a watch, which he wound each night before sleeping and each morning when he awoke. He once had a belt, until the ants devoured it. On the door hung a top hat, made of wool, and likely not to their taste.

Outside the house was the clearing, where he fought back the philodendrons. The German had planted a papaya tree, and to this Pascal added a patch of yellow watermelons. From the station, the telegraph wire snaked through the little garden and up a foot-worn path to the railway cut, where it climbed a tall pole encrusted with bromeliads, and joined the 608 kilometers of coiled copper that connected the Commission to the Mines. Another small path dropped from the clearing into a lagoon, where every evening, after carefully checking for caimans, Agent Pascal folded his suit on the bank and slipped naked into the black water to bathe.

How had he, a Frenchman, arrived at such a lonely post deep in the jungles of Brazil? Unlike most of the other Line Agents, who were fleeing something in that world populated by other people, he had nothing to run from: no debts, no secrets, no angry cuckolds, no warrants, no corpses left in the wake of knife fights in the tango halls of

Buenos Aires or the harder quarters of Belém. He'd come, he decided, like a pebble tumbles, from Aix to port and port to ship and ship to sea, settling at last in this repose. If during his childhood he had never sought solitude, neither had he sought company. Born into a family of twelve, later sent to study with an order of friars who had taken vows of silence, he had, at one point in his life, either been satiated by the society of others or inoculated against their absence. That he was somehow a different kind of person was a fact that had dawned slowly, during long walks through Aix's Roman quarries and daydreams beneath the river willows and, finally, at sea. When the offer came to fill the post left by the German, he had the sensation of a great expanse opening before him. It was only after the Commission Agent repeated for the third time that Pascal would have to do without the proximity of other people that he realized he was being warned.

Was this the secret of his duration: the presence of a fortitude? Or the absence of a fear? And yet the truth was that in the earliest days at Urupá, it hadn't been so easy. Then, waking very early, he had thought the slow tick of the clock toward 0600 almost unbearable, and as the evening clatter began to die down, he had dreaded the moment when the Line went still. In the garden, tending his melons, or repairing tears in the thatch, he would hear the telegraph tapping and rush inside, only to discover it had been a feint of his imagination. But as the first week gave way to the second, he found himself settling into the days, the heat, the squalling of the insects, the space. By the time the Commission invited him back to Cuiabá for a week in civilization, he responded less with relief than with a vague annoyance that his idyll had been disturbed.

Still, he went. The train was the same that had brought him to Urupá. Lurching, it broke through the vines that had grown across the track. Over swamp and hill, through tunnels of green, past encampments of scattered rails, arriving at last, after three days, to the city on the river, with its sweltering sunlight and its muddy crosshatch of streets.

There he joined a group of Cuiabá officers in their revelry. They were a different kind of men, incapable of solitude or silence, drawn to the jungle for its decadence, its untended maidens, its forests fecund with fruit and game. They must have recognized a reluctant bacchant in the trim little Line Agent, for they loosened his tie and pressed chipped cups of cane wine into his hand. And so he drank with them until the company became unbearable, and then he fled.

By the river, alone, he was approached by a woman in a long white nightgown. At first she seemed some kind of spirit, insubstantial, which was why, perhaps, when she offered him her company, he rose and followed. There was a shack adorned with tattered ribbons, with a planked floor that creaked beneath their feet and a bed made out of scavenged rail ties. When she lifted the chemise above her head, he thought, I will return each year to her. But when she touched him with her fingers, he felt something dangerous in the tenderness, as if he were passing perilously close to a zone of fracture, which might suddenly give way.

The next morning, daylight pouring down over the streets, over the red, earth-stained men, the red horses fat with worm, he'd left her and gone straight to the train station. It was empty, so he waited alone in a dark corner while a mangy dog gnawed at its tail with fury. Rain came, hammering against the tin. In the evening, an engine appeared out of the jungle, steaming, seething, festooned with torn foliage like some exhausted reveler at a Rite of Spring. Three days later he descended at his station house, where he found the melons ripe and close to bursting.

After that, he never returned to the city. He knew this troubled the Commission. Too often they had seen agents drift into that particular languor of the jungle, that listless melancholia that roughened into a frenzy as the forest walls closed in. Please let us know when you would like to come to Cuiabá, they wrote him—at first a gentle suggestion, later more of a command. It is highly recommended, they said, for body and spirit, for hygiene of the mind. To these requests, Agent Pascal replied politely, deferring each time for a few more months. But inside, he found himself protesting. What was he, still a child, told to come and play with others? Couldn't a man find peace and happiness at rest inside his little room? Why did he need the city when he had the other Line Agents? Wasn't that true friendship—not some night of carousing in Cuiabá?

For the truth was that, however distant his colleagues were, he'd come to understand them intimately over the years, could describe each man, each station, with details he had never seen. From their requests for medicines, he knew that Pinto, at Várzea Nova with his wife and daughter, suffered lumbago, that somehow in this land of dysentery Brother Perez was chronically constipated, and that the Hungarian at Juá, a defrocked pharmacist who variously spelled his name S-z-a-r-s-a-l-y or S-a-r-s-z-a-l-y, drifted in and out of fevers, perceiving faces in the leaves and voices in the humming of the Line. He knew their heights and weights by their instructions to the tailor, their favorite foods by the rations they requested, the relative meticulousness of their grooming by their calls for shaving razors or cologne. He followed the education of Bonplan's daughters through the Latin primers ordered by their father, the oldest already on to vocatives and second declensions. By the reports of visitors, or Indians, or claim jumpers, or deserters from the penal battalions, he knew what each agent thought of other men.

Officially, the Line wasn't to be used for anything but matters pertaining to the Mines. And while most of the men obeyed, others seemed unable to resist the lure of gossip or debate. Of these, the two Argentines were the worst: Fernandes and Brother Perez, different as wool and water, and yet inextricably entwined. Fernandes was a cardsharp, a debtor who was hiding from his creditors and confessed petty thievery in the manner of a man who'd done much worse. He was thin and tall and, according to Szarsaly, who had seen him, very handsome; in Cuiabá, the Commission officers described his adventures with a bit of awe. Frequently there came news from the Depot that a certain Edviges was asking after him. Other times, an Ana Maria. He had a common-law wife, Mathilde, the daughter of an English tailor, whom somehow he had lured to his godforsaken site. It was she whom the bulk of his requests concerned: magazines and bonbons, and silky undergarments, described in detail. One year, Fernandes spent his entire bonus on a phonograph. Another, he ordered little waistcoats for a pair of capuchin monkeys they kept as pets. He was routinely late in his transmissions, blaming it on "calisthenics," which Pascal took to mean Mathilde.

And Brother Perez? A fat man, to judge by his trousers, and a rashy one, by the quantities of talcum that made up his supply. He, too, was not alone, having established at the Mines a kind of personal mission, preaching to the miners from Saint Ignatius's *Spiritual Exercises* and bribing passing tribesmen with the same bonbons Fernandes ordered for Mathilde. When not proselytizing to the local sinners, the brother turned his attentions to the other agents, and in particular Fernandes, who—as Perez often reminded the kilometers of copper that tied them all together—was shaming Argentina by unsanctioned copulation. To which Fernandes replied with even more requests for lingerie, including the most exacting measurements of Mathilde's thighs and waist and breasts, as well as detailed reports of where the last delivery had pinched too tightly, the pink marks the elastic left upon her skin.

And Perez: I would remind us all that there is a special circle in hell for common-law husbands Stop

And Fernandes: Waist 33 now 44 around the buttocks plumper on the breadfruit Stop

And Perez: Recall the eternal fate of Paolo and Francesca Stop

And Fernandes: Paolo who? I don't recall that agent. Was he before my time? Stop

And Perez: Fornicator

And Fernandes: Rechecked. 34 and 45

And the cycle of denunciation and exposition would repeat itself with such regularity that Agent Pascal began to suspect that such loving descriptions may have been the true incentive for the Good Brother Perez's denunciations from the start.

Sometimes the men shared recipes for cakes or manioc and tapir stew. Or palm wine. Or jungle goulash, conceived by Szarsaly at around the time he started going mad.

They also shared their miracles. The snake that bit without envenoming, the blade deflected at a bar fight in Cuiabá, the tree split by a lightning strike, sparing the fragile little station and its sleeping agent. When Bonplan's second daughter had presented breech and two weeks early, they all listened as his wife went into labor, all powerless to help. Then, Bonplan had ordered his older daughter, scarcely two at the time, into the garden lest she be forever haunted by the image of her mother's death. In hindsight he would admit this was a mistake, but at that moment, in such raw panic, he wasn't thinking of what might be lurking in the dark. He was hammering at the telegraph, begging for a doctor, pleading, *Someone, someone tell me what to do,* when the door opened and his daughter entered, holding the hand of a tiny person bedecked with beads. He couldn't tell if it was a man or a woman. He assumed she—he—it—had come from a tribe of Indians that migrated through nearby hunting grounds, but they were shy, and until that day, none had ever ventured beyond the edge of the clearing. Later, the Hungarian would say it was a manifestation of the Boldogasszony, an old deity who in his home country helped women in difficult childbirths. Perez would claim it was the Blessed Mother herself. For the rest of the night, none of them could sleep, imagining the child resting in her exhausted mother's arms.

These, then, were Pascal's friends: the good patriarch, the pharmacist, the sinner, and the priest. And last, of course, was Wilson-Jones. Though they had never met (indeed, Agent Pascal had never met any of them in the flesh), he reserved a special place in his affections for the Englishman, the only other agent to have lived so long alone. Fernandes had Mathilde, and Perez had Saint Ignatius, and Pinto and Bonplan had their families; even the Hungarian had his hallucinations. Yet from the day of his arrival seven years prior, replacing a mutinous Belgian, Wilson-Jones had endured without a single visit back to Cuiabá.

Of the man's life before the Line, Pascal knew virtually nothing. Unlike Szarsaly, who betrayed his nostalgia by a seemingly irresistible need to compare the local food and weather to that of Hungary, Wilson-Jones had never even uttered the word "England," mentioned neither wife nor mistress, gave no clue as to his prior profession. He, too, had simply tumbled there, thought Pascal, who found something immensely reassuring in this company, as if the other's solitude sustained his own.

And yet there was more to his fondness than the symmetry of their conditions. Briefly, at the beginning of his time in Urupá, Agent Pascal, malarial, discovering that the ants had infiltrated his quinine, had sent a request for resupply, a common appeal and one not worth remembering, except that two days later a train traveling back from the Mines had stopped at Urupá to deliver a small bottle of tablets, which the conductor said had come from "the agent at Canaã." There was no note, no well-wishing, and yet despite this, the act stayed with Hippolyte Pascal. Indeed, years later, alone in his hut, or walking along the rail and staring at the ever-encroaching forest, at the high wire slung in great loops from the tall poles shaped like beggars' crutches, he found himself marveling at this realization that he could live in the thoughts of another person, a realization that seemed no less a miracle than if somehow he'd been twinned. In his rare moments of doubt—not loneliness exactly, but a simple awareness of space and distance, of infinity and eternity; not fear, just a brief shiver, a shifting in his repose—in these moments, Pascal imagined himself in the mind of that other man, 262 kilometers forward on the Line. Just as he imagined that Wilson-Jones, when he felt his head grow dizzy with the space and light, sought comfort in the meditations of his friend Pascal.

He kept the bottle long after he had swallowed all the tablets, though he knew that simple courtesy dictated its return.

What else might he say of Wilson-Jones? He was tall and a bit paunchy to judge from his tailoring, liked flowers, reveled in descriptions of the metallic shimmer of the palm leaves and the pink that bloomed in fluted starbursts out-side his room. He liked to read, and the names of novels filled his requisitions to Cuiabá. An odd and futile demand, thought Pascal, for the nearest bookstore was on the other side of the Andes, unless one counted the itinerant peddler who sold the primers to Bonplan's daughters and the moldering magazines to Mathilde.

Once, it occurred to Pascal that instead of returning to Cuiabá for rest and relaxation, he might take the train forward, to Canaã. Then, beneath him, the earth moved, and he did not consider it again.

And so the years passed. The heat, the screeching of the insects. The vines lengthening in their infinite coil. The clouds and trains. The telegraph tapping, tapping. So regular was the sound, the code of names and stations, that it felt as much a rhythm of his own body as his heartbeat or his breath. He wondered if the others felt it, too, that same pulse, as if they were all a single organism, a Hydra, like the swamp reeds connected at the roots. There was little to distinguish one day from the next, little, even, to mark the direction of time's arrow, save the advance of Bonplan's daughters through their lessons, or the slow descent of the meniscus of his mustache oil. He woke and slept with the sun, which, because of his proximity to the equator, bisected his hours into equal portions of day and night. By the end of his first year, his dreams had taken on a similar regularity, recapitulations of his waking life, down to the syncopation of a dream telegraph, the taste of dream melons, the fragrance of dream lavender. Indeed, so symmetrical were the hours that he wondered whether it might be possible to con-fuse his two lives, though, oddly, in his dreams, the forest was blue and the sky was green. Why this should be was a great puzzle to him, and occupied hours of consideration. In that other life, as in the waking one, he was alone.

Mostly alone. There were moments, beneath skies both blue and green, that he sensed a presence behind him as he attended to the signal. And once, he had dreamed—yes, certainly it was a dream, for a soft green light was falling across their faces—that all the men, Pinto and Bonplan, Wilson-Jones, Szarsaly, and the two Argentines, and their wives and children were walking together, single file, through the cut. In the dream, someone was speaking words of comfort, though he couldn't understand them, and hadn't known he was afraid. Someone was singing. He saw the priest, his cassock swaying, and Mathilde, a capuchin in her arms, and Bonplan, sweeping up one of his girls when she grew tired. And though the vision was of nothing more than people walking together, there was something about it that was painfully beautiful, and he hoped and feared that it would come again.

In his sixth year a rumor circulated that the Mines might close, and with them the telegraph. For two months he expected every train to be the one to take him back. He couldn't conceive of leaving the station. He would hide if they came for him, he decided. Hide and remain, as the forest closed around him, living on melons and water from the lagoon. For life, he thought: because once the cut scarred over, there would be no way to return. For life, he thought, and then wondered if he were so distant from everything that even death, loping through the brush with fang and talon, might miss him, might pass him by.

One morning, during the monsoons of his ninth year, Agent Pascal woke to the sun and the sound of parrots, rose from his hammock, dressed, set his kettle on the fire, and sat at the table to check the signal.

At 0600, he received the first transmission from the Depot, followed shortly by the second, from Pinto at Várzea Nova, and the third, from Szarsaly at Juá. Then he replied, PASCAL REPORTS, URUPA, 0600, and waited for the others to answer: Fernandes at Itiraca, Bonplan at Macunarímbare...

But then: a pause. He looked up. A fly circled. Before he could bat it away, the telegraph clacked again to life.

REPEAT: CUIABA REPORTS, 0601

PINTO REPORTS. VARZEA NOVA

SZARSALY JUA

PASCAL URUPA

FERNANDES ITIRACA

BONPLAN MACUNARIMBARE

And then again: silence.

CUIABA REPORTS. CALLING ALL AGENTS. THE SIGNAL IS NOT GETTING PAST MACUNARIMBARE. WILSON-JONES? PEREZ? PLEASE REPLY STOP

Nothing. Ever so slightly, Agent Pascal shifted in his seat, feeling somehow in the flow of seconds a resistance, a tightening in the air. The kettle began to boil. Waiting, fingers resting on the table, he closed his eyes. Before him, the Line stretched forward, nestled in its narrow cut. Through swamp and forest, past the flocks of parrots, the herds of peccaries and tapirs, the tribes of men. Anything might have happened, he thought. A fallen tree, a sabotage. The fact that neither Wilson-Jones nor Perez was answering reassured him. It located the problem not to an agent but to the Line.

Tap tap. Cuiabá again, he thought, leaning back, but then the letters formed. One short stroke, two long, one short. One short stroke. One short stroke, one long, one short. One short. Two long, two short. Perez.

PEREZ REPORTS FROM THE MINES. THE LINE IS OPEN.

CUIABA REPORTS. PEREZ CONFIRMS THE LINE IS OPEN TO THE MINES. CANAA CONFIRM. AGENT WILSON-JONES CONFIRM. IS THERE SOMEONE AT CANAA?

Slowly, Pascal inhaled. On his watch, the second hand swept its depths.

Again from the Mines: PEREZ REPORTS. THE LINE IS OPEN. THERE IS NO ANSWER FROM CANAA

CUIABA REPORTS. CONFIRMED: THE LINE IS OPEN. AGENT WILSON-JONES CONFIRM STOP

The kettle was now gently rocking on its cooking trivet.

PEREZ REPORTS. THE LINE IS OPEN. And again, as if they all needed to hear it one more time: THERE IS NO ANSWER FROM CANAA

Agent Pascal stood, stroking his mustache. It was then that he became aware of a silence, an impossible silence, as if the crickets, the screaming birds and monkeys, had ceased in unison. There is something outside, he thought. But he didn't move. He could hear his breath, fast and deep. There is nothing wrong, he thought, or spoke, for now he heard his own voice, coming from somewhere in the room. *There is nothing wrong.* Many times agents had been late for their transmissions. Perhaps ants had gotten into the telegraph, or prospectors had stolen the wire, or Wilson-Jones had simply forgotten to wind his wristwatch and was savoring his morning bath. Perhaps he had returned to the country he had come from, to the life, the people, of whom he never spoke. Scarcely three minutes had passed.

Again, the telegraph sounded: again, the Depot. Again, the others answered. Pinto, Szarsaly, Pascal, Fernandes, Bonplan.

A pause. Perez.

Three times this repeated, the answers like ripples settling over water. The telegraph went still. Now in the silence and the shadows, Pascal could see them. The agent at Cuiabá, rising solemnly to share the news with the Director. Pinto, unmoving, as his wife eyed him from the hearth. Szarsaly, shivering inside his blanket. Fernandes, naked on the wooden stool, ignoring the worried caresses from Mathilde. Bonplan's girls, ceasing in their play, wide-eyed, not daring to ask the question. Perez, in his cassock, finger on the hymnal. All, like Pascal, waiting and watching their identical zinc and copper dragons, waiting for the thrum of life.

An agent isn't answering, Pinto says to his wife, in Várzea Nova.

Go back to playing, Bonplan tells his girls. *There's nothing wrong.*

The Hungarian rises to decant a concoction for his distemper.

A rivulet of sweat gathers at Mathilde's clavicle.

Suspice, Domine, whispers Perez. *Oh Lord, receive.*

At Urupá, Hippolyte Pascal stood in his doorway and stared into the wall of green. I cannot worry, he told himself again. But now these words found little purchase. He had been a Line Agent for nine years, and he knew well the ritual that would follow: the soldiers sent deep into the forest, the wary approach to the silent station house, the agent found pierced through with spears or arrows, or hanging from the beams. Or simply resting, cocooned in his hammock, already blooming with mushrooms, half eaten by the ants. Though mostly, he knew, they found nothing. A door open, a room empty, clean. Eventually, a new agent would arrive, and for some weeks the detail would remain there, guarding the station, until at last the men grew sick of one another, and permission came from Cuiabá for the soldiers to return.

On the table, the dragon lurched. Urupa confirm, said

the Line, and Pascal realized that for the others along the wire, he, too, had disappeared.

ARE YOU THERE? the Line asked again. For a moment, Agent Pascal found himself uncertain what to say. Then through the forest came a surge, of something great and wondrous heaving past, and he sat and smoothed his mustache and he answered that he was.

ON THE CAUSE OF
WINDS AND WAVES, &C

My Dear Sister,

I do not know if and how this letter will reach you, but I must have faith that it will find a way. Haven't we all heard tales of shipwrecked sailors carried home by the currents? Or messages, stoppered in bottles, that arrive at their intended destinations? And yet even if my words should find themselves lost among the clouds, I still must write, so that the sun might know, and the winds and rains.

I know that ever since my earliest practice of the art of aerostation, you have worried about my safety. When I married Pierre, when he first taught me to fly, when he understood that the public, thrilled by our great balloonists, would be even more enraptured by a female *aéronaute*—so many times you have written of your fears. Indeed, there have been days that I have wondered if I should give up and join you in your simple country life of animals and children and bedsheets flapping in the yard. But *something* has driven me skyward; it feels as if each choice I made was not my own but guided by that steady hand called Fate. Even my baptismal name has felt like some hint of destiny. Perhaps this may offer you but little comfort; perhaps such words may worry you even further. Then just know this: your Céleste is well, in health, and not alone. Indeed I might call myself the luckiest woman in the skies.

I believe it was last February that we corresponded? Your letter—telling me about the harvests, your children, the beauty of the winter in Charleval—arrived shortly before my eighth flight, in March. By then, the controversy that had attended my first ascents had all but vanished. Certainly, there were those still grumbling that with all the brave men taking balloons into the sky, there was no need to expose the more delicate organs of the fairer sex to the dangers of speed and changing air pressure. But there were few in Paris who had not been charmed by my skill, my daring. How the dull costumes of M. Blanchard or Doctor Jefferies paled in comparison with my silks! You have read of the processions that greet me before each flight, the tens of thousands of spectators, the celebrations in song and paint. I have sent you the many whimsical snuffboxes and bracelets, the chest pieces carved with my likeness, the plates that bear my face!

Yes, the eighth flight promised to be no different. The

day was the sixteenth, the weather clement despite the frost that lingered on the ground. We had launched from the Champ de Mars, before crowds so great that spectators were knocked into the Seine. My ascent was flawless, the winds brisk and without guile, and after circling the city, I was being carried toward the north when, not far from Pontoise, I found myself approaching a heavy cloud bank. Having flown in clouds before, I saw no reason to desist, but rather decided to investigate its interior. Dropping ballast so as to rise inside it, I was instantly struck by the quality of the mist, so thick I might have carved a piece out of it, and tinted with pale amber, as if it were a great alembic in which the sun had been distilled. I worried briefly that the balloon would collect too much water, but when I tossed out a fistful of feathers, they showed me to be rising, and at last I broke above the clouds and emerged beneath a great expanse of dazzling sky.

It was, I realized with a glance at my instruments, higher than I had ever flown before (indeed, higher, I would later learn, following the calculations, than *anyone* had flown). Seized by a sudden vertigo, I was making to start my descent when a strange vision in the distance caught my eye. It appeared at first as a fine line, declining from the highest reaches of the sky, but as the currents began to draw me closer, I had the sense of an unevenness about it, like a crack across a vessel, or a tear in silk. Of course, this was ridiculous! A crack? A tear? And in what? And yet the impression was undeniable. By my estimation, it was about as high again as the altitude of my balloon, too fine, too inky black to be a cloud, and yet too gigantic to be anything of terrestrial origin that might have taken flight. I have seen extraordinary things in all my travels, all kinds of mirage and atmospheric phenomena: cloud halos, double rainbows, crests of vapor crystals, shooting stars. But nothing like the strange sight before me.

Until then, a gentle southerly had been carrying me toward this vision, but as I drew closer, the wind began to slowly shift direction. I tossed out a bag of ballast, seeking some higher corridor, waited, then dropped another. But now I stalled. *Higher then!* I thought, and released another bag of sand, and then my last. But... nothing! Oh, it was as if the skies themselves had sensed my curiosity and wished to hide their secret! And then I was swept away, and swiftly. Panicking, I pulled the valve on the balloon, too fast, and dropped beneath the clouds.

Inside again, and no longer transfixed by the strange vision, I realized, with a start, the peril of the situation I had placed myself in. At such a height, and now without a single teaspoon of sand with which to jettison if I so needed! I had only one direction to go, Thérèse, and that was down. Indeed, another fistful of feathers confirmed what I suspected from a sense of weightlessness—I was descending quickly, and now through angrier currents, swift and storming. The balloon, grown heavy with rain, its air cooled and contracting, had begun to fold like a wineskin. Condensation streamed down the riggings in rivulets.

It was a long way through the darkness, and when I emerged again from the belly, I found myself over un-familiar fields—green and dark, broken by emerald patches of winter cabbage. I passed farmhouses and snaking stone walls, dovecotes, streams swollen with the rain. Faster now. A forest loomed before me; I knew I must bring myself to earth before I crashed into its trees. Swiftly I released the gas valve. The ground rushed up to me; I hurled my instru-ments over the basket, the balloon rose suddenly, then fell, shredding a path through a sloping field of barley. I threw my anchor—it caught—I lurched back—the basket struck. But someone must have been watching out for me that day, for as I was thrown forward, I was caught—cushioned—in the deflating silks of my balloon.

Oh what a sight I must have been for the villagers who found me! My pink gown torn and muddied, my limbs tangled in the riggings, my great aerostat stretched out across their fields like some stranded cetacean, expiring its last breath. My strangeness was probably all that saved me from bloody revenge for the great swathe I'd cut through their barley. Yes, there were still some who might have murdered me with their scythes, had not, to my great fortune, a schoolteacher arrived, a follower of aerostation, who counted a print of my sixth flight among the favorites in his collection. I had crashed in the Vexin Français, he told me, near the town of Ivry-le-Temple, some twenty leagues northwest of Paris. A cart was summoned. Balloon and balloonist were gathered up, and after a night in the schoolteacher's home, generously attended to by his wife and sister, I was taken by a second cart to Paris. There, after two days' journey, I was greeted with jubilation, news of my arrival having been sent on ahead.

Pierre was among the crowds that came to meet me, as relieved at my having survived as he was thrilled by the story the crash would make. He had wasted no time in arranging for the printing of a pamphlet with Monsieur Mérigot, across from the Opéra. Indeed, he told me, he had sketched a draft already! Now he just needed the details of what had happened on the flight.

But what *had* happened? Before I stepped down from the oxcart, I turned back in the direction from which I'd come. Yet still the clouds hung over us, and I could find no explanation. To appease my husband, I invented an ordinary tale, adding only the twist of bad weather and the crash. But no sooner had I returned home, than I began to search our simple library for books on flight or natural history that might shed light on the phenomenon. At last, Pierre, finding me one night asleep before a pile of open tomes, pried the story from me. I told him everything: my boldness, my folly, the vision.

I was afraid, given the strangeness of the story, that he would doubt me, mock me. Instead, he listened, rapt, a smile spreading across his face. Had he heard of such a thing? I asked him. Had he, before he retired from ballooning, ever seen such a sight himself? But no, he shook his head. I could search all the volumes in the world, he told me, and find nothing. No, not since the ancients had man dreamed of a tear in the firmament. Perhaps, he said, we had been wrong to abandon the lessons of Ptolemy and Aristotle. Perhaps there was no sun, no moon, perhaps the sky *was* but God's curtain, and I had discovered no less than an open seam.

I didn't know whether to take him seriously. God's curtain? And before what stage? Of course I had no proof myself that the heavens were structured as described by Kepler or Galileo; I simply took it on their authority, as did any reasonable woman or man. But among Pierre's faculties, Reason had always played a second to Imagination, particularly when Love of Lucre was involved. And so I was not surprised when, two days later, he appeared in our foyer with a perspiring Monsieur Mérigot, the latter lugging some two thousand new pamphlets, reprinted *With a New Appendix Detailing a Most Magnificent Discovery.* What I was not prepared for was the request that came but one week later from the Académie des Sciences, inquiring about the "puzzling claims" I'd made, of certain "physical and optical phenomena of the upper atmosphere," and asking that I appear before their body one month hence.

I was terrified, of course. I still had no explanation for my vision. And I was aware of how few women had ever been called before the Académie. Nervously I joked to Pierre that the rare appearance of the fairer sex within its chambers suggested a danger to our delicate organs far greater than the upper atmosphere. But my husband was utterly delighted. By then we had sold out of the second printing, and he had released a third, devoted "to the science of the phenomena above the clouds" and stuffed with shoddy natural history, hazy metaphysical speculation, and a lot of rehashed literary mush. It, too, sold out.

And yet, despite my annoyance with my husband, by then I had become so troubled by the memory of my vision that I held out hope that at the very least a visit to the Académie might provide me with some kind of explanation. After much consideration, I selected a subtle dress of cream-colored silk, elegant and restrained, befitting a serious emissary of the clouds. Pierre, however, urged me to dress *à l'aerostat*—to wear my flying costume, which, he assured me, would not only delight the members of the Académie, but thrill the press. At last we settled on a compromise: I wore a sky-blue robe *à la polonaise,* with its great bunched-up skirts and tasseled bodice, though with white petticoats instead of pink, and a more modest neckline. My hair I placed in simple curls, without the great nest of bows and ribbons I wore on my flights. I also refused Pierre's request that I cover my shoulders with a sable sash "to symbolize the rent in the firmament." My *testimony,* I told him, would suffice.

As it happened, it did not suffice. Rising before that august body to report my observations, I quickly realized that I had been invited not to embark on some shared inquiry, but rather to have my observations—no, my entire person, my honesty, my honor—called into question with such vehemence that my skin burns, my pulse quickens, to think of it even now.

It happened quickly. I was about a minute into my address when there arose a cough of protest from the gallery, and Monsieur the Secretary interrupted my narration. "We have read the pamphlets, *Madame,* there is no need to repeat them here," he said. "If you wouldn't mind some questions..."

Of course there was no way for me to refuse him. One by one he called upon his colleagues. One by one they rose and looked down to the place on the dais where I sat. How was it, they asked, that this *body* was so great that I had to crane my neck as I described it, and yet it had never been observed from earth? Were the people of the Vexin Français so bound to their terrestrial tasks as to have never once looked up? And if it was a tear, a rift, a rent in the heavens, what was I proposing lay behind it? It was well known that the higher atmosphere caused travelers to grow giddy; was it not possible that the air above Ivry had caused a little *ivresse,* a little drunkenness? Or had the exhalations of the Vexin plain conspired to *vexe* my mind?

And so on: I claimed to have ascended higher than my

previous journeys—and yet I didn't record my observations? What calculations did I use, anyway? As Deluc had shown, they weren't simple . . . And even *if* I had seen it, even *if* we were to trust my eyes, then why would one assume it was anything but an odd-shaped cloud? Why, just the other day (said one Docteur Guyot), I saw a cloud shaped just like a poodle! With this, the esteemed chamber descended into esteemed silliness. A sheep! A cow! *My* little boy sees ships! a fourth one shouted. A fifth claimed—outlining the shapes with his gnarled hands—that he'd seen great globes shaped like Madame Guyot.

I knew then that they never expected any answer. I tried to respond, but the hilarity over clouds shaped like women's bottoms had consumed the august fraternity, and only ended with a stern rap of the Secretary's gavel. This time he spoke not to me, but to Pierre. This was a dangerous game *Madame* was playing, he intoned. For nearly three centuries, Science had toiled to tear Earth from the farcical core of a Ptolemaic cosmos, but there were still forces that would have us back there. In his mind, only one question remained about my testimony: whether the thinness of the air had deceived *my* faculties of perception, or whether—and here the room was utterly still—"you've come intending to deceive us."

Thérèse! You can imagine the humiliation. To have gone to them in the spirit of shared inquiry, only to be accused of either madness or charlatanism! To have fallen so far that they addressed their verdict to my husband! My face burned. I instinctively attempted to draw up my décolletage, which only drew more attention to the ridiculousness of my dress. But for all the anger I felt for the Académie, my wrath burned brightest toward Pierre. No, if not for his buffoonish showmanship, I still believe my claims might have been taken seriously. For what respectable woman of science appears before the Académie and claims to have discovered a tear in God's fabric while attired as if going to a masquerade?

At home, a winter settled between us. Pierre pleaded, brought me sweets and ridiculous trinkets. All great explorers were met with mockery, he told me. Think of Commodore Cartier, he said, or Captain Cook!

Cartier thought he had discovered *Asia,* I said. In Canada. Cook was dismembered by the Sandwich Islanders.

"As I said."

"Pierre."

"*Céleste.* Go back."

"Back?"

"Another ascent."

"And how would *that* make anyone believe me?"

"It won't," he said. "But if someone accompanies you..."

I forced a laugh. "They will believe *you* even less."

He made a bow as in acknowledgment. Of course, *he* couldn't be trusted. But then who would join me? Given the fervent interest in ballooning, one would think it easy to find a second pilot. But we needed a learned, sober man, a true *philosophe,* and the problem was, as we'd learned long ago, sober men don't usually take flight. And following the scandal at the Académie, I knew that any reasonable person would worry about the effect on his reputation. Indeed, while the public interest in my "revelation" showed no sign of abating, our more serious friends seemed suddenly quite scarce. Two weeks passed. We had begun to grow disheartened when we received a letter from one Étienne-Polycarpe de La Rochemartin, Marquis of that ancient estate, a known patron of the sciences, a painter, and author of *On the Cause of Winds and Waves, Precipitations, Sea Currents, and Other Atmospheric and Oceanic Phenomena, &c,* who had recently returned from a geologic and artistic expedition in the Apennines of Abruzzo and learned of our plight.

We met in June. He arrived at our apartment not by carriage but on horseback, dismounting in a great swirl of cap and cape. Despite the celebrated circles into which my ascents have raised me, I have found that most of my interactions with the aristocracy leave me but sharply aware of my coarser origins. But if I was prepared for yet another nobleman who spoke only to my husband, I was certainly mistaken. For no sooner had the Marquis risen from his grand bow than his eyes found mine and never left. Indeed, for such an esteemed man of learning, Rochemartin seemed vastly more interested in my person than in any of the philosophical questions of our flight. "Yes," he said as Pierre spoke about the purpose of our mission; "Mm-hmm," said he when Pierre described the technicalities of preparation; "Yes, of course," said the Marquis when Pierre proposed a day to fly. He made no comment on *any* practical matter. When he did speak, it was to convey his *joy* and *honor* at being able to serve as *the humble factotum to such a creature,* and that he could *only dream* of what visions we might find from such a height, &c, &c, his insinuations growing even more brazen as he saw how I blushed. Of course, I was not for a moment flattered, although given his sky-blue eyes and skin still glowing from the Abruzzo, I can imagine that a less serious woman might have fallen for him then and there. If anyone, it was my husband who seemed smitten. Pierre, whose cleverness often overwhelms his moral judgment, clearly saw an opening in our friend's enchantment. With various stratagems more befitting a bordello madam—feigning concern about the giddy effects of altitude on the female mind, promising the greatest airborne *ecstasies,* &c—he secured not only the Marquis's participation but complete funding of the flight.

I left the meeting in a new fury, as much at my near whoring as at the thought of the risks posed by flying with such an ape. Pierre waved this all away. He had little worry about my ability to tame my would-be lover, he told me. I should be grateful. The Marquis, for all his lechery, was not just wealthy, but a scholar; I might learn a thing or two reading his treatise on the winds.

And he painted! Yes, that very evening, he sent a servant back with several of his paintings, thick with garish daubs of *cuisse de nymphe émue,* indeed thick with the nymphs themselves, caressing each other in different settings: a glen, a seaside, a mountain stream. The paintings were actually much better than I expected. Granted, he was no Fragonard, but try to get Fragonard up in a balloon.

We laughed at this one for a while.

Pierre raised a painting of two very pink Egyptians bathing each other at the foot of the pyramids. "Did they really use *bars* of soap back then?" he asked.

With this I relented. Joking aside, by then I was desperate for the chance to return to the skies. The date of our departure was set for the morning of July 23, four weeks away. Because of her great tumble in March, the balloon was in dire need of repairs, all of which were facilitated by the Marquis's generosity. To better control the direction of our flight, we added a *moulinet*—a sort of propeller, recently innovated and much praised. Pierre, meanwhile, set about procuring iron and vitriol for the production of the gas, selling post-flight interviews, and overseeing the printing of new postcards and pamphlets. For these he commissioned a singular image from our usual engraver, showing me in the basket of my aerostat, staring at that inky rift. Of course, the artist had taken the usual liberties with my figure, tousling my hair with an amorous flourish and lowering my neckline to a latitude that scarcely would have served its retaining function on earth, let alone in the jostling of a balloon. If I was annoyed by the exuberance with which the illustrator enjoyed my bosom, this at least I could excuse. Not the accompanying poem.

> Ye gentle Iris of the skies
> Who brings such visions to our eyes:
> On Zephyr's wings fly ye into the rent
> Of the Holy Firmament!
>
> What shall ye see?
> Will angels' wings caress your trembling breasts?
> Or witness ye, that place of our eternal rest?
> Or will ye find in that most secret place
> The vision: God's immortal face?
>
> What scenes await, we cannot know!
> What sky-seas, what clouds as white as snow!
> But know this, maid, if ye shall not return again
> Our loss will be but Helios's gain.

"Helios's gain?" I shouted. In other words: If I die? And the angels could keep their wings to themselves, thank you. But it was the line about God's face I most objected to. Had I *ever* made such a claim? I hadn't even said it was a "rent," just that it *appeared* so. This had to stop, I told him. I understood that interest needed to be generated. But now I didn't know whether the men of science or of faith would hate us more. Even Saint Joan, blessed as she was, heard only the voices of the *angels*. And I: God's face?

Pierre laughed. "*Ma chérie* . . . my sweet confection . . ."

"Your confection!" I answered, hurling a souvenir tea-cup from my fifth ascent. He dodged; it smashed against the wall. He caught me, kissed me. We had tickets to sell, he said. And tickets, *chérie,* were sold to people who believe in heaven, not in physics. Hadn't I noticed how the Marquis seemed to be spending a disconcerting amount on decorations? There was a real chance we might run out of funds.

The worst of this was that Pierre was right. The cost of iron alone could bankrupt us. And the past had taught that certain benefactors, especially the most extravagant ones, were men of many fickle commitments and often illiquid wealth.

Fortunately, there was little time for my humor to darken further. At last the week was upon us, then the day. While the balloon and basket had been transported to the Tuileries the prior evening, I was not to arrive at the launching grounds until shortly before our scheduled departure, so as to deny the people the object of their adulation until their impatience could no longer be contained. Strangely, waiting alone at home, I feared that in place of spectators I would arrive to find the balloon grounds empty, as if the day, as if my life so far, were a great hoax created by a force beyond my view. But at last the carriage *did* arrive, and stepping from our door and into the street, I heard a faint tinkling, a drumming, which, as we approached, grew louder and louder, until it drowned out the creaking of the carriage and the clopping of the horses' hooves. Eight times I had done this, and eight times it seemed impossible that such celebration could be for me. But soon the streets were so crowded that my driver had to stop and call for the gendarmerie to clear the way. We inched forward, turned a corner, another, until at last we reached the Seine.

And there she was. Fully inflated, her pink silks decorated with stars and mythic ships, the fleur-de-lys, the lion-headed serpent from the arms of the House of La Rochemartin. Even the oars and blades of the *moulinet* seemed to glow in the late morning light. Surrounded by the cheering crowd, heaving in her moorings, she reminded me of an untamed mare. But no matter how majestically she loomed above us, once the crowd was alerted to my presence, they forgot her and turned to me. Now, despite any forebodings, I could not but lose myself in the exuberance that surrounded us—the children clamoring to ride alongside me, the ladies staring at my clothes in envy, the brazen men who tossed letters of admiration through my open window. How easy it was to simply surrender to it all, the cheers, the songs, the horns and wild costumes as if from Carnival. I was drunk, I will admit. Drunk—and even before I reached Pierre, now waiting upon the great scaffold beneath the billowing silk, a trumpet in one hand and a bottle of champagne in the other, fumes of sulfur rising around him from the vats that fed the final drafts of gas into the balloon.

I descended from my carriage. The crowd hurled itself forward; the gendarmes fought them back. A postcard and dripping quill were somehow pressed into my hands. I obliged a signature and, on returning it, fought to withdraw my hand from an unseen pair of lips. I mounted the scaffolding to find myself at last before the Marquis. There I stopped to take him in. Despite the extravagance of my dress, his costume was of a resplendence that made mine look like a widow's mourning. His coat and tights were sky blue, his shirt golden as the sun, with frilled, golden ruffles suggesting sunbeams; his cravat was pink as sunset. Great waggly tufts of cotton in the shape of clouds were sewn about his chest and leggings. His plumed hat, tilted at a jaunty angle, was sculpted in black velvet and speckled with glittering white gemstones—the stars! And everywhere, his clothes were embroidered with replicas of our sky-ship. Even his shoe buckles bore little metal aerostats, perfectly replicated down to the oars and *moulinet*.

It was as if someone had designed them with the intent of catching on rigging or punching a hole in the wicker of the basket, I told him. Even from a distance I could smell his perfume.

He smiled seductively. I ignored him, and turned to the crowds. I have always enjoyed the merrymaking, and yet that day, I dallied even longer. Was it the warmth of the summer morning? Or the contrast between this gay reception by the people and the Académie's cold mockery? Or was it my desire to assert some power over Rochemartin? Or something else, some sense that once the winds whisked us upward, I would be at the mercy of a force, a Mover, much greater than myself? Indeed, Thérèse, since I was a child, I have sensed that I was somehow chosen, that a course was set for me, that the freedom others spoke of was simply an illusion. I have felt at times like a doll who, waking into the world, cannot understand how she came to be so gaudily dressed. Do you recall, Thérèse, the plays we used to perform as children, and how, perversely, I would change my lines? Looking back now, I wonder if that too was not a revolt against this sense of predetermination. People speak of the terror of the unknown, but the unknown has never frightened me. The more freedom I seek, the more I feel bound up by fate, by expectation, as if I were nothing less than someone else's creation. A confection, indeed! I've sometimes even wondered if my escape to the skies could be said to represent a testing of this fantastic script that life has written. For there are few moments in which one gives oneself over to fate so completely as in the air.

Ah, but I had little time for such thoughts! I boarded. A child leapt onto the stage and followed me inside. With a kiss on his little nose, I handed him back to his mother. I checked the riggings, the propeller, flourished the oars, now hurrying a little, for the crowd was nearly mutinous. There was a fanfare. A messenger arrived from the Court with a note from His Highness, wishing us Godspeed. Then at last, with nothing left on earth to retain us, I sent up a small balloon, and watched it rise slowly to the east over the city, before a swifter wind carried it northward. At sixteen minutes after eleven, I ordered the cords untied. The balloon surged. The crowd overcame the scaffold, and for a moment I was certain it would drag us back into its maw. Thinking swiftly, I pulled a fistful of glittering ribbons from my hair and threw them into the waiting hands.

We rose. Burdened with two bodies and our equipment, the start of our ascent was slow and stately, availing us a grand vision of the mass of well-wishers who swept out along the quay. There is an extraordinary moment, Thérèse, when one is high enough to take in the rooftops, the expanding city, and yet is still close enough to make out individual faces in their stunning variety—the fat and thin, the long-nosed and pointy-chinned, the cross-eyed, the toothless, the pale, the cherub-cheeked, the bald, the hairy, the jowled, the joyous, the frightened, the awed—until the balloon crosses a magical threshold, and the mass of people merge into one great body, whose dreams seem to rise together, carrying you higher into the sky.

Thus was my state of mind as we took off: thrilled by the magic of flight, and yet still utterly sober when it came to the seriousness of my responsibilities. No, I had no doubts as to the probity of my senses. My city lay beneath me. A cool breeze caressed my skin. The familiar smell of sulfur lingered about the basket, mixing with the pleasing odor of silk warming in the sun. On my lips I could still taste my sip of the champagne. As for the faculty of friendship, I could not help but turn to the Marquis, who, at least for that brief moment, seemed to have forgotten me, and was craning so far over the side with his telescope that I think he would have lost his wig and hat had they not been pasted to his head. "Notre-Dame!" he whispered, giddy as a child. "And that garden must be Luxembourg, and look at all the little boats in the Seine! They are like the toys I played with as a child! Such joy! Oh, dear Monsieur Blaise was right: it *is* containment which causes our unhappiness. And there, Les Invalides...!" As I watched him, my opinion couldn't help but soften, a little. It *was* extraordinary; it had never ceased to be. And a companion, a *co-visionary,* however buffoonish, was a companion nonetheless.

We rose higher, now entering the southerly that had carried off my test balloon. The city retreated swiftly behind us. The first clouds appeared, delicate at first, then thicker. I jettisoned our first bag of ballast, then a second, as we ascended along a wispy cornice like a pair of celestial mountaineers.

It was now forty minutes after eleven, and already I calculated that we were some six leagues beyond the site of our launch. I was, of course, still dressed only in my gown, which, for all its beauty, was hardly fit for the requirements of keeping warm. Indeed, in this respect, the Marquis at least was better insulated. Ahead of us, a high bank of clouds stood between us and our destination. Wrapping myself in a shawl, I suggested that we start making measurements. Were we to rediscover that strange heavenly body, we would need a detailed atmospheric record to appease our doubters. And so while I began to take down readings from the barometer and thermometer, and marked the types and positions of the clouds, the Marquis set about ordering a set of small flasks that he opened at various points during our ascent, so as to capture samples of the air. He was, I will admit, proving a far better assistant than the rutting monkey I had first suspected he would be, and as he went about his way, I felt I could fully direct my attention to my work without fear that he might mount me if I turned my back. In addition to the flasks, he had brought along various other scientific instruments, some of which he showed me, measuring the electricity about my person with an electrometer, and capturing my breath in an aerometer, to compare it to the weight of wisps of cloud through which we passed. Every once in a while, he would stop his experiments and, without explanation, scribble a few words on a little sheet of paper, address it with a flourish, kiss it, and then cast the letter overboard, watching with his telescope as it fluttered down.

As I have noted on earlier flights, the heavens, far from being the empty space most men of earth imagine, are in fact traversed by life both great and small. No sooner had we begun our experiments than we found ourselves attended upon by a flock of pigeons in their grey livery, and when these visitors had departed, a pair of goshawks circled, squawking in curious admiration. A little farther along, butterflies fluttered past, and soon we were showered in a veritable battalion of little balloonists—a spray of spiders streaming on their own aerostats of thread!

Delighted, I turned to my companion. "Look," I said, catching one of the little pilots on a gloved fingertip. The spider hesitated briefly before beginning to make his way up my arm, crossing brazenly onto my skin. He would have progressed inside my shirtsleeve had the Marquis not removed one of his gloves and gently touched my arm above the elbow, letting it linger while the spider climbed onto his thumb. With a brief puff of his breath, he sent it on its way.

I laughed. He turned and bowed, and for a moment, absurdly, I thought he might ask me to dance. He moved a little closer. "Your shawl," he said, and gently lifted it back into place.

I looked off into the distance. He said, "How you remind me of a young woman I once met!"

"Oh yes?" I asked, my eyes drawn back to his, annoyed to note that, against my wishes, a tinge of envy had crept into my voice. "And is it to *her* you send your letters?"

A forlorn look came upon his face. It had been on his last expedition, he said, to find the great city of Crocodilopolis once described in Herodotus. For months he had marched through the desert, nearly dying of thirst, at last forced to sacrifice his camels for food. He had made it to Upper Nubia, near the Sixth Cataract of the Nile, when he was captured by slave traders and conveyed across the desert to the sea. It was there that he met her, a girl with eyes like amethysts, and skin as dark as mine was milky white. They shared no common language, but through the intervention of an old woman who spoke both Arabic and the girl's tongue, he came to love her and learned that she was to be sold to a vizier of Jiddah. He had planned to escape with her, to carry her to Paris, but when he went to find her the next morning, she was gone.

Given that I did not believe a word of this ridiculous story, I didn't expect to find myself so touched. To my surprise, a tear rolled down my cheek.

"My dear," the Marquis said, quite tenderly.

I wiped my eyes. Then, almost as if another was speaking for me, I added, "There are times when I too feel as if I am no longer the mistress of my fate."

The curls of his wig waved softly in the wind, the pink of his cravat cast a warm glow over his skin. I thought of some of the words he had written in his book, on whether it was "the wind that caressed the wave, or the wave that stroked the belly of wind."

"Let's eat!" I said.

We sat. Beneath his seat, the Marquis had stashed several bottles of wine from his estates, and offered to pour me a glass while I removed my gloves and set about preparing some pâté. But only one, I said, for we must not sully our observations; wine was so much stronger at this height. If the Académie doubted my observations when sober, what would they think of them if I were drunk? "Of course!" said Rochemartin with a twinkle in his eye. "To the Académie, then, the bastards!" We toasted. We sipped, toasted again. I handed him his plate. He said something, which I imagined to be Latin, but, given the heavy-lidded way in which he said it, I decided not to ask for its translation. He finished his glass with a single gulp. "A kiss?"

"Marquis!" I exclaimed. Oh, but why did I not move away?

A smile played over his lips. "If only to study the effects of high altitude on the functions of the heart."

"The *heart,* Marquis?" I asked, slicing a baguette.

"A *philosophical* investigation," said he.

I smiled. "Yes? And if I should be curious about the effects of bread knives on the—what did you call it—*heart*?"

"My Aphrodite!" He gulped down another glass.

His hand, my thigh.

My hand, his hand, away. Oh, the charade! As we were but players in light comedy! But still I did not move.

Again his hand.

This time I let it stay.

I waited for him to move closer so that I might push him from me.

"Céleste!" he implored.

I didn't answer.

"Céleste!"

I lifted my face.

"The *sky,* Céleste!"

Ah yes, *the sky.* For behind me, the clouds had dropped away, revealing, in the shimmering distance, that great black line. "The *rift,*" murmured my companion. "It is... of course..." For now there could be no doubt about it. Oh, how I had restrained myself back on earth, how I had tried to confine myself only to description. But even at this distance, it was clear that the sight that met our eyes could be nothing else but a tear in the very fabric of the heavens. Instantly, Rochemartin lifted his telescope to his eyes. "Astounding... I had never..." But if he was about to say that he had never believed my vision, I didn't know. For it was as if someone had taken our voices from us. Before us, the clouds parted further. We moved swiftly, the great black slash rising ever higher in the sky.

On earth, imagining this moment, I had resolved not to turn back, whatever the winds. I would toss every instrument, I told myself, draw on the oars with every ounce of strength, if only to pull closer to my goal. But now as we approached, the wind continued in our favor, as if the rift possessed its own magnetic force. The closer we came, the wider the body of the rent. By comparing it to the distant clouds that seemed to pass before it, I estimated that at its widest, it was perhaps some two hundred meters across, but tapering at both ends, as fractures in an earthen vessel taper, to the very fineness of a single hair.

We came closer. We were lower than I had expected. Jettisoning ballast, I nudged us higher, then higher yet. Still there was utter silence. I let loose two bags of sand. Up the undulating line, we rose. We had no destination then. We merely stared, marveling at the strangeness, the sable depths that lay beyond the tear in the sky. From time to time, we turned the *moulinet* or stroked the oars to keep us closer. The Marquis, like me, I knew, was trying to see inside it. I realized now that up close, the edge of sky had the texture not of fabric but something more substantial, more fleshlike, like a thin torn piece of potter's clay or the rind of a melon. And within, some kind of substance, liquid, glistening and dark.

We came to a halt, suspended in the ether, perhaps half a league along the fissure's course. Below I could see the fields of clouds passing over the French countryside. In the distance: the great curve of the earth, the sea. I knew that I should take recordings to describe our height, the pressure and moisture of the air, but I could not bring myself to tear my eyes from that shimmering darkness, as if at any moment something might emerge out of its depths. And then, no sooner did I have this thought than something did.

A drop, a single black drop fell out of the rift above us and landed on the back of my wrist, still bare from when I had removed my gloves. Slowly, I lifted it, as the Marquis leaned in closer. Before our eyes, the drop trembled. We watched. The surface broke and there emerged a spider, identical to that little flier we had seen below. A thread unspooled into the atmosphere, caught the faintest air current, and drew the creature into space. For a moment, we stared out in wonder, before turning back to the remaining shattered droplet on my wrist. Slowly, gently, the Marquis raised it to his lips, to taste.

"It's ink," he said.

But I knew this. For that which can make a spider can also make a balloon, a telescope, a marquis, a sudden understanding. Can write the clouds, the winds that suddenly began to stir again.

And so we fly on, through earth's sweet exhalations. How many days have passed, how many months, or years? Below, armies cross the plains, and herds of wild horses. We see cities grow, smoke streaming from their rooftops. Ships knock up against each other alongside the quay; the straits stream with great schools of whales. We sail over pyramids, and forests blooming with scarlet flowers. From jungle tree-tops, men with long bows fire arrows at our silhouette.

How long will I remain aloft, Thérèse? Alas, the one who knows the answer has kept it hidden. Tomorrow, will he capsize us upon a deserted isle? Or return us to the softness of our beds? Or will he have us float forever through his ink-well, until the final page is written and the book is closed? If we are all confections, then the Confectioner gives no sign. For now, we find ourselves provisioned by a wine bottle that has no bottom, a basket that replenishes itself with food. For warmth: each other. I sit and watch the skies and write this letter, as I in turn am written, read.

Adieu, Thérèse! The heavens turn, we hurtle into night. Snow falls on the retreating mountaintops. The moon appears, ships climb up from the earth and settle on her plains. With the seal of the Marquis I close this letter and toss it earthward. Will it reach you? Will it drift down upon the currents, to Boreas, to Zephyr, and, tumbling, flutter down a thousand leagues to where you stand gazing up amidst your flapping sheets? Impossible, of course, but so we all are. How swiftly we are summoned up, and on!

A REGISTRY OF MY PASSAGE
UPON THE EARTH

Beginnings. 22.December.1938 Midnight, accompanied by seven angels on clouds shaped like a stairway, they left me at the house, at the base of the walls.São Clemente Street.number 301.Botafogo.Rio de Janeiro, I alone with lance in hand.

I was born in 1911. In 1911, there was yellow fever in Leblon. In 1911, the Monk José Maria began to preach the Holy Bible in Paraná, a man touched the South Pole, the kingdom of Machu Picchu was discovered. In 1911 there were ships, not my ships but steamships with masts like cigarettes. I registered 1911 with 19 cigarettes and 3 forks each with 4 prongs, 1 prong broken. I wrapped them in blue thread.

In Sergipe, where I was born, washerwomen lay clothes on the banks to dry. They dry fast, they turn stiff, they Crack when shaken, one of the four sounds of clothing.

When I was a sailor, nothing dried. In Sergipe, where I was born, there are clay houses.cacti.skeletons.skinny goats. vultures circling.

Exhibit. Banner, embroidery in five colors. Blue.Red. Grey Blue.Black.Light Blue. Images of Life in the Navy. Images of bicycles.drum sets.horses. 12 horses, all embroidered.

Exhibit. Banner. Depictions of life in Colônia Juliano Moreira (Director's House.Pavilions.Patients walking). Notably absent is the name Rosângela Maria (Intern). It is an early work, before she came.

Exhibit. Sculpture. How I would make a wall. I would shatter glass and put the fragments teeth up in concrete. You must keep your house safe from the insane and from salesmen.

Exhibit. Collection of Buttons. So that God will know of buttons, and how they were.

In the year of the yellow fever I was born in Sergipe. In Sergipe I spent my First.Second.Third.Fourth.Ninth. Twelfth.Thirteenth birthdays. On my Fourteenth birthday, in the Chapel of Our Lady of Tears, I heard God's voice, and with it the voices of the Virgin Mother, sweet and soft like the lady in Rio who sells fried pastry at the Colônia, who gave me *coxinha* the day I came to the gate in my Cloak of Presentation. That day I said, I heard your voice before. It can't be, she said, I've never met you. No, we met years ago, I said. She waited, looked past the gate to the pavilions, said, Where, *filho?* In heaven, I answered, You spoke without your corporeal form. She crossed herself. Never tell anyone, she told me. She still comes for me. She sends me buttons.clothespins.pieces of string. I find them scattered about the yard in clever and strategic places.

On my Fourteenth birthday, God said, You are my Servant. I looked everywhere, but there was only my mother praying.the priest praying.two others.no one else.

Exhibit. Collection of Sandals and Sieves. 3 sieves. 20 sandals. 9 with straps. 11 sandals without straps. 1 bottle of clothespins. Here I register the 9 ways man walks toward things and the 11 ways he flees.

Memory. In the little church of Our Lady of Tears was Blandina Francisca Bispo (Mother). Also Jesus with a broken hand (plaster) and Our Lady (plaster), her face wiped smooth. They said in Sergipe, Touch her eyes and she will do your weeping for you. There were four pews. two doors.one wasp flying high in the rafters. God said, Pay attention. His voice was very loud. He said, Arthur, you are my servant. I looked around. I thought, No one else can hear.

When I was fourteen and two months three weeks exactly, His voice again came from the cane. He said, You are my Prophet. He said, Put seven pieces of cane in the sand, order them from smallest to largest. I did this. Then he said, Cut six pieces and order them from bluest to yellowest. I did this. There was silence. Perhaps this won't be so hard, I thought.

Later the foreman found them. What are these? he asked me, Were you stealing? Pick them up right now. I can't, I said, I will be punished. He said, Son, I will show you punishment. I was crying, I knew there would be trouble, but I couldn't move. He grabbed my shoulders. Don't mock me, he said. I wanted to say, I am not mocking, but from somewhere a voice said, There must be order in the world. He must have thought it came from me, because he raised his fist.

Exhibit. Collection of straw hats left by visitors to Colônia Juliano Moreira, Jacarepaguá, State of Rio de Janeiro, founded in 1924 as the Colônia de Psicopatas, eighty square kilometers, with jaboticaba trees.papaya trees.great swinging mangos. Where have lived 3784.3573.2948.3121 patients, including Jacinto Bastita das Neves.Armando Binto. Ivo de Brito.3781 others, organized by doctors onto note cards, with salient characteristics so they may sort them swiftly and with ease. Including one Bispo do Rosário, Arthur, black, single, origin unknown, literate, no family, police record, paranoid schizophrenic, of which five are lies and three are truths.

★　★　★

From my room at the asylum, I can see the mountains.palm trees.swinging mangos, the yard where the other patients walk.crawl.hover hummingbird-like, meters above the ground.

Some are very sick. They have skin ulcers.tuberculosis.tremors, they snap their fingers, they talk when no one is there. There were times I was like that, talking talking. I don't remember much from that Epoch of My History. Not all signals are understood on first reception, one must have the codebooks, the semaphore of God is vast.

Exhibit. Banner. 18 ships I have seen during my passage upon the earth. Including Destroyer.Battleship.Merchant Marine.Steamer. 18 ports including Rio.Bahia.Santos. New York United States.Panama City.Fortaleza.Natal. Features of each city. A list of men and their professions, beginning with six of many held by Arthur Bispo do Rosário. Cane cutter.Sailor.Boxer.Employee of LightIndústriaBrasileira.Doctor.Ambassador of God. Illustration of such professions. Illustration of 16 Navy insignias. Illustration of chess-sets.compasses. I represent Nations and their flags.

In Sergipe, where I am from, I ran from the foreman and into the cane. I stopped. I heard only my own breathing.crickets.nothing else. I heard, Arthur. I heard, Everything is wrong, there is no order. I said, Where are you hiding? I slashed at the cane around me. Come out! I told it, You are making me crazy, I will lose my job.

It said, Easy, son, we all have a burden. Stop talking, I shouted, Show me where you are talking from or I will beat you to a pulp. Look into the brush, it told me. I walked until I found a *caatingueiro* and shook its branches, and a piece of wood fell out, shaped like Our Lady. I picked it up. I was trembling. I waited, but there was nothing else.

At home I put it above my bed. My mother said, What is this stick? Your sin, something said, and she looked down at me, with worry. She put her hand on my forehead. She said, You quit the fields. The bastard foreman was going to hit me, I said. The foreman is your uncle, she told me. He came because he is worried. I saw her mouth moving, but a great rumbling rose up in my ears.

Exhibit. Names of women, so that God will know. Josefa. Luísa.Ana (Intern).Lourdes.Conceição dos Santos (Doctor). Eugênia (Nurse).Izabel.Maria.Celeste.Rosângela Maria (Intern). Embroidered in blue in circles inside my Cloak of Presentation. It is what I will wear on Judgment Day, when I fast and dry out and make myself transparent, to appear before the Lord with my Registry that shows the world of men. It is one of many works to include the Names of Women. It is the most important, with the name Rosângela Maria (Intern), who helped me complete my organization of souls.

She said, Arthur, it is a most exquisite cloak. It reminds me of a king's robe, a boxer's mantle. But tell me first about the man inside.

Exhibit. Banner. Life in the Navy. School for Naval Apprentices. Illustrations of classrooms.libraries.gymnasium for physical culture. Where parents bring their sons they have great dreams for and sons they can't control. Not depicted is Adriano Bispo do Rosário, father, who signed the papers with an X. Also not depicted: Blandina Francisca (attack of weeping.left behind).

Is he healthy? asked the recruiter. Any history of injuries, evidence of insanity, disciplinary problems? He's not too young?

Fourteen, I thought. Sixteen, my father said. I thought, I should correct him, but beyond the men, light was moving against the ocean in ways I hadn't seen before.

Exhibit. I recall the fallen. Names of 232 sailors encountered on my passage, among them Luiz Eduardo dos Santos signalman.Hipólito Páscoa signalman.Private Antônio Nunes repairman of torpedoes. 229 others, embroidered by Arthur Bispo do Rosário, sailor, collector of lives.

Exhibit. List of jobs held by Arthur Bispo in the Navy. Cabin Boy.Signalman.Helmsman. Forms of signaling mastered. Shape signals.Motion signals (semaphore.wigwag).Heliograph (from shore only).Night signals (four lamp ardois.winker.semaphore with light). Forms of pennants. Letter flags.Numeral flags.Repeater flags.Telegraphic flag (red over white, diagonally split). Important signals (Disabled Ship. Ship Quarantined.Brasil Expects that Every Man will do his Duty.Anchor Down.Man Overboard). How to spell this in hand semaphore and sinister hoists.

You are quite the scholar, the Captain told me, But you should go on shore leave with the others, You should relax. Yes, Captain! I told him, but at night I slipped away with the signal book that I had taken with me. Inside there was everything that needed to be said.

Exhibit. Banner. Embassies of all Nations and their Qualities. Arabia.Cuba.Italy(Pisa.Volcano).Gabon.Egypt (Pyramid.Pharaoh).Yugoslavia. Embroidered in thread pulled from my clothing, on bedsheets taken from the asylum (white.stained.pavilion stamps). Sometimes I would stitch so much, the ideas so fast, that I was left with but a single sleeve. It took years for the nurses.doctors.guards to understand that I was not like the other patients who tore their shirts off because they thought them straitjackets.poison.bees.fire. That if I had proper materials, I would happily preserve my clothes.

Exhibit. Banner. Map of Brasil. All the kinds of shapes conceived by man's geometry. Triangle.Square.Hexagon.Quadrilateral. All stitched in blue (bedclothes), save three small dogs in black.

On my trips across the sea, I sorted and organized the clouds. I made three categories. Clouds shaped like ships, Clouds that rain, and Other. From Natal to Lisbon, I also sorted them by the speed they moved, by Clouds that Cast Shadows, and Clouds that are Avoided by Seabirds. I sorted the quality of light on the water into Green-Blue.White.Glass.Green.Other. I organized the fluttering of winds in sails. There were fourteen emotions experienced by sailors on the ship, eleven by myself. I did not experience Anger.Voluptuousness.Disgust. This was my first attempt at sorting something one cannot see. It was a difficult project, before Rosângela Maria (Intern), but in the end I was pleased.

Chloral hydrate.haloperidol.chlorpromazine.thioridazine. fluphenazine. If they were pills I hid them high in my cheek and spit them out in the garden like little bird droppings, beneath a soon well-tranquilized tree. If they were injections I shouted, clinging to memories at sea.

I sat with the doctor. He said, Bispo, you were a signalman, a sailor. I said, I was a sailor.boxer.prized employee of LightIndústriaBrasileira.bodyguard.panner of gold. He said, When were you a sailor? I said, In 1925 I joined the School for Naval Apprentices, I left behind Blandina Francisca, My new mother was Maria de Jesus. He said, And how long were you in the Navy? Eight years, I told him. And how many years were you a boxer? Eight years. I was Lightweight

Champion of the Navy. Yes, I heard that, And when did you come to the Colônia, Arthur? Tell me again, I'm new here. On 22 December, midnight, accompanied by seven angels, I presented myself before the monks at the Monastery of São Bento, Rio de Janeiro, it took 1938 years to get to Botafogo across the heavens, I came to the Colônia by bus. That is quite a journey, said the doctor, I hope the roads are not as bad throughout the heavens. I wouldn't know, I told him, Through those I sailed.

He stopped and smiled. He said, Tell me again, Arthur, why you left the Navy? Your papers say that you were always fighting, always in trouble, they say that you were court-martialed under Article 41, for "moral turpitude," Why was this? I wasn't court-martialed, I told him, In the courts of man, perhaps, but not the courts of heaven, There is a difference in jurisdiction. He laughed again. There is, my friend, there is.

He paused again. Fourteen is young to leave your family, Arthur. Did you ever see them afterward? Was there trouble even back then? That's young for problems such as yours to start.

Arthur? he said. Fingers touching his desk.his tie. his beard. Arthur? Legs crossed.uncrossed. *Arthur.* I saw behind him the shadows of tree branches. I noticed four types, man-made shadows.branches.leaves-not-fluttering. leaves-fluttering. I made a note to record them in blue thread.

★ ★ ★

Exhibit. Banner. Activities in the Navy. Forms of Rest and Relaxation. Calisthenics.Boxing.Tug-of-War. Names of fighters. Baltazar Cardoso.Annibal Prior.Tio Teodoro.Kid Pepe.Thiago Burk. Nicknames given to Arthur Bispo, Lightweight champion. Sea-Wolf.The Bronze Mariner. You can hit me, but God made me like granite and you will only break your hands.

They put me in the brig for fighting. Also for lassitude. Also failure to comply with regulations regarding uniforms, for my shirts that were too silky and for my resplendent shoes. At my hearing, I said, I am Lightweight Champion, you can read about me in the papers. That is not the issue, replied the Captain, The issue is comportment, If you represent the Navy, you must obey the Navy's rules. I said, I fought Kid Pepe.Baltazar Cardoso. You could fight the Devil, he told me, but you would still have to wear your uniform when you go on shore. Who said anything about the Devil? I asked him. He looked to the bailiff, who took one step toward me. Easy, sailor, said the Captain, No need to get upset. Who said anything about the Devil? I demanded, Don't lie, God made me like granite, Don't put words into my mouth.

From my ship, I fled into the city. It was winter, misty. Somewhere, men were following me. There were Corpo-

rals.First sergeants.Corvette Captains.Admirals. In the skies
I watched for signs, studied the semaphore of street busk-
ers, the wigwag of policemen, the Morse of traffic lights,
I evaded capture by the guards of Pilate and by midship-
men, first-class. When it was dark, I went into a bar with
music (samba.*choro*.Josephine Baker). There were men who
danced with girls with lipstick.frilled skirts.perfume.curls.
Above the bar were hundreds of bottles of cachaça. There
was Good Times.Cuckold's Consolation.Passionate Indian.
Forget Your Troubles.Willing Woman. I drank water, then
Forget Your Troubles. Freedom must be celebrated, even the
terrestrial kind. When the world was spinning, a girl came
and took me to a room with a red bulb.magazine photos
of women.dirty sheets.shelf (empty glass.Our Lady of Sor-
rows.plastic flowers.book with torn spine). When we lay
down she said to me, You are not normal. I didn't answer. I
was busy cataloguing her expressions. There was Abandon-
ment.Loneliness.Love.Violence, she wore them on her face.
She touched me. I said nothing.waited.watched her move
above me, a movement between a ship at sea and grass
swaying, above weeping and below laughter, somewhere to
the side of joy.

I ran again. I lived in doorways.a shack of wood.be-
neath the bridges. In the day I registered the comings
and goings of the city, and my passage through it. No
one saw me. If I needed money I found gloves-off *50 mil
reis* fights out by the dockside. What an uppercut! they

told me, but I didn't tell them who I was. Once a man struck me with a ring and my color turned vermillion (eye swollen.fever.heat.shaking). I stripped my clothes and went to drown the fever in the water. I slept in the sand, and dreamed of the girl with lipstick, woke with an erection from the sun and a woman screaming. I heard, Pervert, felt boots on me, heard, God, Look at his eye. I catalogued the different footsteps and their sound in the sand as they walked away and back and picked me up in a blanket and carried me.drove me.threw me into a room, where for three days I tried to shout over the angels. Then they came and beat me.kicked me until I stopped. Scales fell from my eye, the red one, and I could see.

The angels cried, You are missing your work, your duty! Let me alone! I answered. I whispered, Please let me alone, please, they will never let me go if you keep talking. The next day they opened the door into the street.bright light, and I immediately began to make an Inventory of the cars that were passing in the Rio sun.

At Juliano Moreira, I stand in front of a mirror (scavenged.diagonally split). I see my coat, its ribbons.buttons.thread. I see the room.chipped whitewash.shadows. carts filled with my Registry. I cannot see myself, I am invisible. It is a glorious coat, with many details.

Others can see me. I know what they see, I have recorded their whispers. Outside, when I get permission to leave the grounds, I see them move away from me across the street.

Rosângela Maria (Intern) looks and says, I see a boxer, a sailor. I say, I am invisible. You are, she says, The most visible invisible man in Brasil. In the world, I correct her, turning to look at the back of the cloak. I represent the world.

Exhibit. Kitchen Utensils. Metal Cups.Metal Plates.Metal Trays. All used by inmates.patients at Colônia Juliano Moreira. Part of Registry of Daily Life, Series.

It was summer, warmer. I stayed away from the dockside matches, God told me I could rest. I bathed in the sea. At Carnival, I danced with a girl in feathers (peacock.parrot.raven) before the crowds whisked her away. I went back to the bar to look for the girl with the lipstick.frills, but she wasn't there, only another who was like her. This one asked for payment first. She said after a while, You going to do anything with me? On the shelf, the statue of Our Lady of Sorrows had been replaced by a statue of Padre Cícero of Juazeiro, who also hears the words of God. She lowered the straps of her dress and let me put my palms on her shoulders. They were warm. I let my hands rest on her warm shoulders, and I thought, Oh no, now God will ask for a registry of different kinds of warmths, but the angels were quiet, perhaps they were also enjoying Carnival. She asked, Is that all? I didn't answer. Okay, she said, Each to his own, You're not the first nut I've ever met.

I saved coins from carrying crates to ships that sailed the seas I sailed in. I worked through the night and earned the wages of two men. I rented a room. I bought a blanket that I folded over. Never have I slept on anything so soft. The room had a view of a wall and a tree with a thousand shadows. I collected stones from the sea and laid them over the floor. I organized them by size, and by color, by angles and the presence of bumps and ridges.

Once, I sat outside and saw a man working on a telephone pole. I asked him questions. Perhaps, he told me after a long discussion, Your future lies in Electricity. I saw the challenge and the possibilities. I followed him to LightIndústriaBrasileira, responsible for electrifying the nation of Brasil.

Here I note twelve kinds of Warmth, Blankets. Sun.Wood Burning.Paper Burning.Jacket.Summer.Stove. Feijoada.Tea.Sand.Stones.Shoulders. Think about how to depict this in embroidery with blue thread.

At Light, I began by cleaning tramcars. It was not the work I had imagined, but sometimes the ways of God are hidden, one must retain one's faith. I worked at night, scrubbing the floors and windows until they were gleaming, and in the day I dreamed of the places they had gone and the people that they carried. From the garage at Largo dos Leões, webs of electricity spread out across the nation. I could see it, feel it powering the trams, pulsing, carrying signals to the darkest reaches of the Amazon, broadcasting across the seas.

The manager came to me. A man was needed in Tire Repair, he told me. Tire repair? I wondered. I was once Chief Signalman.Lightweight Champion of the Navy! He took me to Viação Excelsior, to the great hangar that held the buses and the trams. This is your man, he told the foreman. The foreman brought me to a table. These are bolts and nuts and washers and wires we wish to use again, he told me, I need someone to sort them out.

You work in clever ways, I said to God, but said it only in my mind.

Exhibit. Daily News. Here I collect the important occurrences of the age:

Teresina City—Piauí State—Maria Antônia Pereira da Silva, 22 years of age, killed her friend with two stabs in the chest—The Victim was Maria de Jesus do Nascimento—26 years—Hours before she had stolen a chicken.

Monica Pereira Dutra—15 years—is missing from her house on Neripi Street 303—17 December 1988.

Killed her Boss to Rob her—Jurema Rangel Pereira— The victims were Onovalda de Souza Manso and José Barreira Manso—30 July 1986—the bodies buried at the farm.

Also included in exhibit: names collected from newspapers (16 Sandras, from Sandra Cristina to Sandra Teixeira, also the names Jeane.Solange).

The doctor said, Bispo, if you are recording history, you are missing the launching of men into space, the elections of presidents. Why do you record so many stories of poor girls who have been lost or murdered? But I only bowed in answer. My room was filling up with newspapers, and there was little time left to sort the names.

At Viação Excelsior, I sorted the pieces by color. At the end of the day, the foreman came to me. He laughed, No my friend, not color! I should have explained: by type! By type? I thought. Of course not! But I said nothing. I stayed the night and by morning I had ordered my table and the one beside me. The foreman came again and looked at me like there was something funny. Well, my good man, I must have gotten lucky, it is hard to find such enterprise these days.

Next, he said, Bispo, you'll box these axle parts, they are due in Fortaleza by Saturday, I need them packed by the Quality of the Shadows Cast.

I worked through the night. I sat each before a beam. I sorted them by Shadows that Replicated the Object Illuminated.Novel Shadows.Shadows in the Form of Beasts or Women.Shadows that Revealed an Underlying Truth. The next morning, the foreman came. Bispo, what is this? he said. I sorted the parts, I told him, like you asked. He said, The boxes are completely jumbled. Did you remember what I told you?

Farewell! I said. But this one followed, faster, faster.

Somewhere a noise was growing, a great rifting, as if the fabric of the world were tearing in half. I felt the presence of a machine approaching, heard voices shouting, Watch out, Man!, but I didn't turn or stop.

Exhibit. Twos. 2 forks.2 plates.2 tokens.2 dozen pages of daily papers. 2 years spent by Rosângela Maria (Intern) at Colônia Juliano Moreira.

Exhibit. Universal History. Events in the Life. Note the flight from Sergipe. Note the life at sea. Note the flight from the Navy. Note the accident, the omnibus at Viação Excelsior, the foreman shouting, the driver shouting, the right foot crushed to splinters. Note my firing from Viação Excelsior. Note my work as odd jobs man, at São Clemente Street.number 301. Note the approach of 22.December.1938. August.September.October.November.And.

Exhibit. Banner, entitled, How I Came to Earth. Note the seven angels, the clouds shaped like the stairway. Note the pilgrimage to Palácio do Catete, to Praça XV, to the church of Candelària and the church of São Jose, to the Monastery of São Bento, where I announced that I had come to judge the living and the dead.

Note the world and how it is rent.

Exhibits, many. Works dedicated to Rosângela Maria (Intern), who didn't laugh when I gave them to her, who blushed but didn't mind when I said things I shouldn't have said.

She said, What are you trying to repair, Arthur, with so much thread?

Within the White Walls I began with trash. In those first days there were many Doctors and Nurses, they came with medicine that brought clouds sweeping, but still I heard above it all that Time Is Running Short! I wanted to rest, but He wouldn't let me, He who made me like granite, He who gave me infinite strength. I began with wood from market boxes.trash from trash heaps.cloth from bedsheets. I registered Tools of the Earth by wrapping them like mummies in the blue thread from my bedclothes. In an abandoned pavilion by the tuberculosis ward, I built carts to store my representations. The staff seemed puzzled, but some made treks across the grounds to see me. They said, Bispo, What is this? What is that? Sometimes the dullness of mankind astounds me: they held a fork I'd wrapped in blue thread, which held the label "Fork." But soon they began to come with buttons.sandals.dolls.bedsheets stamped and stained.

Others came, from outside. Some saw me on *TV Fantástico,* in the report on the asylum, 1980, also on TV was Cloves de Jesus.Ricardo Serviço.Heraldo de Jesus. Others saw my banners at the art show, the year was 1982. *Margins of Life,* they called it. I did not attend. After the show, in the papers, they argued, Is it Art or is it Child's Play? A Product of Man or Madness? Is it Therapeutic? I clipped the pages and placed them in the bin for Follies of the Age.

I do not answer questions. I do not have time for smaller minds. Even kind people tire me with their ignorant questions. It isn't Art, I tell them, It is a Registry, They are not Exhibits for men, but God, so He may see. A God whose angels wail and howl when I slow down to speak to critics and reporters. If I could have stopped, I would have done so long ago.

The Doctors and the Nurses are people with Wives.Husbands.Families.Homes. I don't want any of this. There is too much work that's left.

Exhibit. Boots of people who have walked the muddy paths of Colônia Juliano Moreira, asylum.

Exhibit. Banner. Two-sided. Embassies of all Nations. Avenida Rosângela Maria.Railways.Train Engines.Signalmen.Avenida de Jesus.

Exhibit. List of names beginning with the letter A. Aristides Langoni, switchman on the Carmo Railroad.Arlindo Eça, breeder of horses, asses, and donkeys.Arthur Rosa, who bled cattle.Alfredo Uales, a good man.

Exhibit. List of words beginning with the letter A. Azul.Aeronauta.Amor.Asma.Arte.Adeus.

Exhibits, in progress. A Registry of Thoughts I've Thought. Of Words I've Heard.

Exhibit. Doormat made with bottle caps. On rainy days, it is used to scrape the clods of clay from shoes.

★ ★ ★

Rosângela Maria (Intern) said, Arthur, here is a book, an Atlas, I found it in the flea market in Liberdade. Hide it under your bed, she told me. Someone might take it if they know you have it, They'll think you're planning your escape.

With the Atlas, I completed:

Exhibit, Miss Universe. 24 banners, Representations of Beautiful Women and their Countries, inspired by broadcast on TV Globo, August 1983. Miss Russia.Miss Israel.Miss France.Miss China.Miss Australia.Miss Canada. Miss Japan.Miss Brasil. Each banner with Features of a nation and its women, Geographic.Economic.Historic. 24 different kinds of Female Beauty. Note thread of 6 colors, all brought to me by Rosângela Maria (Intern.Mender of the World). 200 cm x 50 cm, each attached to flagpole of same length, each pole wrapped in blue thread.

On TV, Miss Spain wins. But really, Rosângela Maria (Intern) wins. She knows, and I.

Rosângela Maria (Director of All I Have) had Brown Eyes.Brown Hair.Hair in Ringlets, sometimes. Her skin was soft like Felt.Down.New Grass after the Rain. I touched her once, only once, only her hand. She sat by a Representation. She asked, What is this? and I told her of my Home.Blandina Francisca weeping. She pointed and asked,

What is this? I told her of the Navy, I told her of the Lightweight Champion. I showed her the ship I'd made for her and me. I called her closer. She told me she was afraid.

I let her go. I shouted at myself, She won't return! But the next morning, she did. She said, Forgotten, forgiven. Laughing.

I was seventy-two years old. I asked, How old are you? Rosângela Maria (Intern) smiled and said, Guess. I said fourteen, seventy-three, sixty. She laughed again and said, Just don't be a mathematician, Arthur. I turn twenty-seven next Thursday.

Exhibit. Registry of items belonging to Rosângela Maria (Intern), given to God's servant between 1981 and 1983. Comb with Strand of Hair.Hand Mirror.Record.Doll. Two jars containing the pieces of two letters. One labeled Goodbye Arthur, One labeled Husband.Baby.São Paulo. This one with torn fragments of a photo, like confetti from a parade.

Before she left, we sat among my representations.
    I said, Maybe I am old enough to slow down.
    She said, I think you have registered everything.
    I said, Everything, I think my work is almost done.
    She said, You could start afresh.
    Like new, I said.
    She said, Just like a child again.
    I said, I am not so busy anymore.

She said, You have time. What do you want most? You have the world, Arthur.

I said, Mother.Wife.Family.Home.

She said nothing. A quiet came on her face, like the quiet that was there in the Beginning and in the End. In it I saw Sadness.Love.Joy.Completion.

MUSICO SEGUNDA CLASSE
A PERNA FICOU OSSO ❭ ALAO ABATE-MEDICO CIRURGIAO HOSPITAL LIOJ
JAPARATUBA MUNICIPIO SERGIPE ❭ ALGUSTO DOS SANTOS-MISSAO
CLASSE CONVEZ DISTROEY 2-PARA ❭ ARTHUR DE JESUS- TERCEIRO SA-
NO-ATENDENTE HOSPITAL PSIQUIATRICO RUA DOTOR LEAL ENGENH
V ANIR BOMFIM-MEDICO PEDIATRA RUA PAULO BARRETO 26 BOTAFOG
ARUJO PRIMEIRA CLASSE SIGNALEIRO ILHA VILLEGAIGNO CORPO MARINH
HEIROS ARACAJU ❭ ALVRO BRUCE- 22-APRENDIZES MARINHEIROS ESCOL
RADA DE FERRO MUNICIPIO CARMO-SERGIPE ❭ APRENDIZES DE MARINHEIRO
RO ENCOURACADO SAO PAULO ❭ ARLINDO TINE-PRIMEIRO SARGENTO EN
DENTRO RUA DOTOR LEAL ❭ AMARAL ESCOBAR- FARMACIA HOSPITAL RL
EY 2-PARA ❭ ARCHILES SALLES-MARUJO PRIMEIRA CLASSE SIGNALEIRO DI
TAO DE MAR E GUERRA COMANDANTE ENCOURACADO FLORIANO ❭ ILHA DO GO
NA ❭ ANTONIO MOREIRA-ATENDENTE NUCLO ULISSE VIANA CENTRO PSI
ANTONIO PINTO-MANOBREIRO ONBUS LIGHT AVIAÇÃO EXERCIOR RUA VOLI
❭ ALUISIO DUTRA-MECANICO EMPLACAMENTO FREIOS GARAGEM ANOITE AVIA
CARMO FIMDA NA RUA OUVIDOR ❭ ABERLADIO ALMINO-PRIMEIRO TENENTE
O NAVIO TENDER BELMONTE ❭ ANTENOR VILELA-PRIMEIRA CLASSE SIGNALE
FOTO ❭ ALMEIDA MEIRELLES-RUA DO PASSEIO 42-LAPA FOTOGRAFO ❭ ALGUS A
TE 277 BOTAFOGO ❭ AMERICO BOLIVAR-RUA BARÃO DE MACHUBA CONSTRUT
EIROS-CABO SIGNALEIRO REBOCADOR-D-DIRETORIA-N-NAVERGACAO-O-OPERI
RO PSIQUIATRICO NUCLO RODRIGUES CALDAS ❭ ARY BATISTA-ATENDENTE N
ALDA-CARPINTEIRO OFICINAS TRENS ARACAJU ❭ ARISTIDES ECA-ARACAJU RES
O COUTINHO-ATENDENTE HOSPITAL PSIQUIATRICO RUA DOUTOR LEAL ENGI
COURACADO FLORIANO ❭ ARMANDO DE OLIVEIRA-CAPITÃO TENENTE ENCOL
ARTHUR TASSIS-RUA VOLUNTARIO DA PATRIA GARAGEM AVIAÇÃO EXERCIOR
NANDES-PUGILISTA PORTUGUES NO RIO 1927 ❭ ANIBAL PRIOR-PUGILISTA POR
MUSICO FOI TRANSFERCIA PARA FUZILEIPOS NAVAES TODA BANDA ❭ ALBINO H
SPITAL PSIQUIATRICO RUA DOUTOR LEAL ENGENHO DENTRO ❭ ALCIDES DUTE
IGADA CORPO MARINHEIROS ILHA VILLEGAIGNON ❭ PSIQUIATRICO AVENIDA P
DENTE NUCLO ULISSE VIANA CENTRO PSIQUIATRICO JACAREPAGUA ❭ ANTEN
ERMEIRO HOSPITAL PSIQUIATRICO AVENIDA PASTEUR PRAIA VERMELHA ❭
MERCIARIO ❭ ARLINDO CARVASARIO-INSPETOR LIGHT AVIAÇÃO EXERCIOR COM
A MUNICIPIO SERGIPE ❭ ALCIDES DOSSANTOS-MISSÃO JAPARATUBA MUNICI
AFOGO COMERCIARIO ❭ ANTONIO LUCAS-MECANICO REGULAGEM DE FREIOS PO
2-PARA ❭ ALCIDES CABRAL-MARUJO PRIMEIRA CLASSE CONVEIS DISTROEY
NDA CLASSE SIGNALEIRO ENCOURACADO SAO PAULO ❭ ARTHUR DILO- SUB O
SSE CONVEIS ENCOURACADO FLORIANO ❭ ARTHUR LOUREIRO-SUB OFICIAL EN
RUJO PRIMEIRA CLASSE ESCOLA APRENDIZES MARINHEIROS ARACAJU SINALEIRO
EDISTROEY 2-PARA ❭ ANTENOR OMENA-MARUJO SEGUNDA CLASSE TORPEDI
GO GLORIA ❭ ARLINDO DE CARVALHO-CHOFE AVIAÇÃO EXERCIOR ONBUS LIGE
-ENFERMEIRO HOSPITAL PSIQUIATRICO AVENIDA PASTEUR PRAIN VERMEL
DO ENCOURACADO SAO PAULO ❭ ANTONIO ROCHA-ATENDENTE CENTRO PSI
RIO BRANCO 183-91 TAVO ANDAS SALAS 808 A 810-EDIFICIO
DISTROEY 2-PARA ❭ ANATACIO AVILA MART

Acknowledgments

For providing the silks and iron needed to get airborne, I am grateful to the National Endowment for the Arts, the Townsend Center for the Humanities at UC Berkeley, the Camargo Foundation, the MacDowell Colony, and Beatrice Monti della Corte von Rezzori of the Santa Maddalena Foundation. For winds boreal: Terry Adams, Robert Alter, Elias Altman, Robert Mailer Anderson, Reagan Arthur, Tom Barton, Nell Beram, Lee Boudreaux, Daniela Cammack, Melissa Chinchillo, Carol Cosman, Robin Desser, Grainne Fox, Sarah Fuentes, Tinker Green, David Grewal, Evan Hansen-Bundy, Lyn Hejinian, Karen Landry, Ira Lapidus, Ashley Marudas, Jed Purdy, Zach Shore, Maggie Southard, Brenda Webster, Elora Weil, Irvin Yalom, and Craig Young. And austral: Roberta Coutinho, Suzana Couto, Tatiano Couto, Samuel Titan; the family of Luiz Schwarcz and Lilia Moritz Schwarcz; Candace Slater;

João Moreira Salles and the journal *piauí;* and Heloisa Jahn, for help with *esteiras* of all kinds.

I will always regret that my passage on this earth never crossed that of Arthur Bispo do Rosário, and his extraordinary work remains an inspiration to this day. Thank you to Raquel Fernandes, Ricardo Resende, and Andrea Bolanho of the Museu Bispo do Rosário Arte Contemporânea for permission to use images of his embroideries, and for your work in preserving his legacy.

Closer to home, I am fortunate to work with inspiring students and patients, and with dedicated colleagues truly too numerous to name; thank you to Laura Roberts for continuing to build within Stanford Psychiatry an atmosphere where interdisciplinary work can thrive.

Thank you to Kevin, Leanna, Max, and Xanthe McGrath for the rivers and the portages; Nathan Perl-Rosenthal for Paris and Charlotte Houghteling for London; Tanya Luhrmann for deciphering clouds and semaphore; Daniel Engber for experimental design; Josh Mooney for the lories and birds-of-paradise; Rafael Oliveira for the slack-water lagoons and entangling bees. *Adiantum, Aspidium, Asplenium, Blechnum, Cheilanthes, Davallia* . . .

As with most collections, several of these stories first hit the scratch elsewhere. I will remain forever grateful for Muscular Ben Metcalf at *Harper's,* who first believed in my short fiction; for the ruby dagger of Chris Cox at *Harper's;* and for the skilled telegraphy of Michael Ray at *Zoetrope.*

One couldn't ask for nimbler Seconds than my agents, Christy Fletcher and Donald Lamm, nor for finer editors than Asya Muchnick at Little, Brown and Company and Maria Rejt at Mantle UK, who know how many times they've freed me when I was tangled in my riggings.

Finally, to the full WrestleMania that is my family: Thank you to Raphael and Peter, Mom and Dad, Ariana, Selah, Debbie, Emma, Fiora, Florence, Susan, Howard, Sylvia, Pearl, Ed, Aaron, Cotton, Betsy and Phil, Bob and Elizabeth. And to Sara, for the fish that leaps within my chest.